P9-CFL-492

By the same author

The Mile High Club
Spanking Watson
Blast from the Past
Roadkill
The Love Song of J. Edgar Hoover
God Bless John Wayne
Armadillos & Old Lace
Elvis, Jesus & Coca-Cola
Musical Chairs
Frequent Flyer
When the Cat's Away
A Case of Lone Star
Greenwich Killing Time

KINKY FRIEDMAN

Steppin' on a Rainbow

SIMON & SCHUSTER
NEW YORK   LONDON   TORONTO   SYDNEY   SINGAPORE

SIMON & SCHUSTER
Rockefeller Center
1230 Avenue of the Americas
New York, NY 10020

For information about special discounts for bulk purchases,
please contact Simon & Schuster Special Sales:
1-800-456-6798 or business@simonandschuster.com

Designed by Deirdre C. Amthor

Manufactured in the United States of America

1   3   5   7   9   10   8   6   4   2

Library of Congress Cataloging-in-Publication Data
Friedman, Kinky.
Steppin' on a rainbow / Kinky Friedman.
p. cm.
1. Private investigators—Hawaii—Fiction. 2. Missing persons—Fiction.
3. Hawaii—Fiction. I. Title

PS3556 R527 S7 2001
813'.54—dc21   2001031159
ISBN 0-684-86487-8

ACKNOWLEDGMENTS

In the final days before Sammy Davis, Jr. was bugled to Jesus, the editor of the *Honolulu Advertiser* assigned star reporter and columnist Will Hoover to write the obit. In a race against time, Hoover completed the obit and turned it in to the editor along with a fairly current photo of Sammy Davis, Jr.'s cancer-ravaged countenance. The editor loved the obit but she hated the picture.

"This doesn't even *look* like Sammy Davis, Jr.!" she shouted. "Go back to the file and find something that looks like Sammy Davis, Jr."

Hoover dutifully went back to the file. Several hours later he returned with a photo, which he tossed onto the editor's desk.

"Now *this* is what we're looking for!" said the editor enthusiastically. "*This* looks like Sammy Davis, Jr."

"Good," said Hoover. "Because it's Billy Crystal."

I dedicate this, my fourteenth novel,
to the woman from India with the
shooting diarrhea.

Get well soon.

CONTENTS

That naughty ol' Sappho of Greece
Said, "What I prefer to a piece
Is to have my pudenda
Massaged by the tenda
Pink tongue of my favorite niece."

—George Holbert Tucker, age 92

PART ONE

On the Blower

Chapter One

The cat was looking at me again with pity in her eyes.

"My heart isn't broken," I said. "I'm just mourning the passing of Thousand Island dressing."

The cat, of course, said nothing. There was nothing much to say. It was the dead of winter in New York and for the first time in my memory all of the Village Irregulars had fled the city. It's not something you'd want to try at home, but it is possible to be alone in New York. As my dearly departed brother Tom Baker once said: "There are worse things in life than being alone." One of them was looking at a cat who was looking at you with pity in her eyes.

"Well, let's see," I said. "Stephanie's on some traditional vacation trip with her family on some private island in the Caribbean where rich people go to laugh. Ratso's out somewhere in Montauk with his black girlfriend Christy who writes for the *Globe*. He's probably busily ghostwriting another autobiography for Howard Stern, which very possibly won't rise to the literary level of the *Globe* but will definitely sell as well."

A slight moue of distaste crossed the countenance of the cat. She did not like Howard Stern. She did not like Don Imus. She did not like Rush Limbaugh. She had no respect for anyone that millions of people listened to. I wasn't sure if she had a point there or not. I was having enough trouble just carrying on a conversation with a cat.

"McGovern's off in Hawaii someplace frenetically gathering

recipes for his new book *Eat, Drink, and Be Kinky.* I'm not kidding you. That's the name of the book. And keeping to a literary theme, believe it or not, Rambam's in Israel going over the manuscript for *his* new book entitled *Nice Jewish Boy (How a Kid from Brooklyn Chased Nazis, Terrorized Terrorists, Made the Russians Nervous, and Had a Good Time).* Hell, even Chinga's out of town. He majored in poetry in college and now he's opening up a new branch of his advertising agency in Miami. He'd better not go too far because he's the only one who can afford to buy any of these books. It just goes to show, you be careful what you wish for, because you're probably not going to get it."

The cat had nodded off somewhere in the middle of my recitation of Rambam's book title, so I contented myself with trying to fire up a half-smoked cigar with a childhood lighter, while staring down at the gathering gloom of Vandam Street. The truth is, of course, you can never really tell whether a cat's asleep or not. It could be merely feigning sleep. It could be dead. Then again, you could be dead. I continued my rambling narrative in the sad, reckless fashion of a man striving vainly to win back a lost lover.

"I ran away once myself," I said. "But you know what happened?"

The cat, who was now lying upside-down on the counter, half-opened one green rather jaded eye. It was obvious that she didn't give a damn what had happened.

"I'll tell you what happened," I said, undeterred by my feline companion's apparent dearth of empathy. "I ran away and then about two weeks later I looked in the rearview mirror and there I was."

And here I was still, I reflected, vaguely becoming aware of my own shadowy image on the windowpane. Here I was, trying to converse with a cat who appeared as if she'd recently returned from a visit to the taxidermist. Here I was, endeavoring to operate a plastic pocket device designed to protect little children and irritate middle-aged amateur private investigators who lived alone in their lofts with their cats, and who, whilst between cases, desired to ignite their half-smoked cigars not to mention their half-dead spirits. Here I was, as Stephanie DuPont had so well put it, "hangin' by spit." She'd been referring, of course, to my relationship with her, but hangin' by spit pretty well described my current relationship with the world. Man cannot live by little Negro puppet heads alone, I thought.

The little black puppet head on the mantel smiled gaily down at me. The fire burned gaily in the fireplace. The world spun gaily around the sun. Maybe I was gay. Maybe that was why most of my friends were men, while women merely scurried rapidly through the crawl space of my existence. Then I thought once again of Stephanie DuPont—that young, five-alarm, acid-tongued Grace Kelly of a woman—and I realized I wasn't gay. I was merely mentally ill to think I had a chance with her. Why would she be interested in an amateur private investigator who was more than twice her age, lived in a dusty, drafty loft with an antisocial cat, and once in a while solved a mystery or two, which usually earned him just enough money to keep him in gourmet cat food and Cuban cigars?

"How often do we find in life," I said to the cat, "that talent is its own reward?"

Since it was a rhetorical question I did not expect the cat to answer and she didn't let me down. Why would any self-respecting cat care about the wonderings and wanderings of a feckless human being anyway? According to the *1999 Calendar and Datebook of the Animal Protection Institute,* a slim document I'd been busily poring over lately, "only two out of ten kittens born in the U.S. ever find a lifelong home."

"Maybe we're both lucky," I said to the cat. "Who cares if we're a little lonely sometimes? Maybe we're lucky to be lonely."

The cat opened both eyes widely. She seemed to be studying me carefully, as if she'd never seen me before in her life. It was not a pleasant sensation.

Now, as the chilly shades of evening fell across the city like a sad little man in an old hotel lowering the venetian blinds, I lowered myself into McGovern's old hand-me-down, overstuffed chair, and poured a strong bolt of Jameson Irish Whiskey into the old bull's horn. I threw a silent salute to the smiling puppet head and threw the contents of the bull's horn down my neck. The cat looked on in mild disgust.

"Friendship's basically overrated," I said. "The Village Irregulars are usually more trouble than they're worth. And women, they're fools, God bless 'em. Anyway, it's down to just the two of us now. We'll get by in this city and this world. They say it's going to snow tonight."

The cat's eyes seemed to melt like old Jewish candles. With that native sensitivity that all cats possess—and all people think *they* possess—the cat once again surprised me with the inexplicable: she crawled over to me and curled up in my lap.

"And now," I said, "if you could help me figure out how to work this goddamn childhood lighter."

Chapter Two

Whenever a detective is not busy solving a mystery he often discovers his own life becoming one. With worldfuls of time on my hands and almost no personnel to spend it with, I found myself masturbating like a monkey on the back of a dying black jazz legend in Paris. The string of successful solutions and colorful adventures that comprised my recent past seemed to mock my current spiritual status, awash on an empty gray ocean of ennui. Had I come this far just to dream all alone? Had I only been treading water in the meaningless mainstream of modern America? I'd spent my time better staying up all night not writing songs in Nashville. I'd had more fun working out crossword puzzles from 1948 British newspapers in a Chinese *kedai* on the banks of a coffee-colored river in Borneo during a three-month monsoon.

"Is this all there is?" I asked the cat one morning.

The cat was busily licking a portion of the female feline anatomy rarely mentioned in 1948 British newspapers.

"There has to be more to life than smoking cigars, drinking espresso, and watching the lewd behaviors of an exhibitionistic, auto-erotic cat. I want to live! I want to paint!"

The cat did not reply. She had the good breeding never to speak when her mouth was full.

This unpleasant, yet strangely riveting spectacle was interrupted suddenly by the incessant ringing of the two red telephones placed at opposite ends of my dusty, disorganized desk. I walked over and picked up the blower on the left. It was Stephanie calling from Nassau.

"What are you doing, Dickhead?" she asked.

"You don't want to know," I said.

"You're right," said Stephanie. "I miss Baby Savannah."

"What about Pyramus and Thisbe? Aren't you concerned that this obvious display of parental favoritism might create some deep anxieties, not to mention sibling rivalries and repressed hostilities toward yourself and your youngest canine companion on the parts of the two older girls?"

"What *are* you doing, Friedman?"

"I'm vainly attempting to fire up a childhood lighter that probably could be operated easily only by a sick child in a Stephen King novel."

"You mean a child-*proof* lighter."

"Depends how painful your childhood was."

"Mine was very happy."

"Well, you know what they say. A happy childhood is the worst possible preparation for life."

"Look, Friedman, I think you're spending too much time alone in that dirty loft with that sick cat."

"That's possible."

"Why don't you go out and do something with some of your friends?"

"I don't have any friends."

"That's a good point."

"All the Village Irregulars are out of town and I'm sitting here—"

"Feeling sorry for yourself—"

"No. If you really want to know what I'm doing I'm—"

"Pouring Miracle-Gro on your dick?"

"Actually, I'm watching the cat licking her vagina."

"I'm warning you, Friedman!"

"That's fucking great. You can say any crude, scatological thing you like, and I can't even truthfully relate what's going on."

"Those are the rules, Dickhead. If you don't like them you can take your balls and go home."

"I don't have a home."

"That's part of your problem. Do you think you could take a moment to talk about anybody else besides yourself? Where, for instance, did all your so-called friends disappear to?"

"Never end a sentence with a preposition."

"Where'd your so-called friends disappear to, Parakeet Dick?"

"Ratso went to Montauk," I said sullenly.

"Good!" said Stephanie sweetly. "Maybe that shark from *Jaws* will bite his dick off."

"Chinga's down in Miami."

"Hopefully he'll be mistaken for a German tourist."

"Rambam's in Israel."

"Trying on yarmulkes or having sex with a camel?"

"He didn't say."

"It's probably sex with a camel then. What about McGovern? He's the only one of your friends that I like. He's a real *mensch*."

"That's because he's not Jewish. He's in Hawaii, by the way. Collecting recipes for his new cookbook."

"What's he calling his cookbook?"

"Eat, Drink, and Be Kinky."

"You've got to be kidding."

"What's wrong with that title? I kind of like it."

"Of *course* you like it. It's about *you*."

"It's not just about me. Everyone from Joseph Heller to Dwight Yoakam is submitting recipes to McGovern. He even said he's getting one from you."

"He is."

"What's the name of the dish?"

"Dick Stew."

"Is it kosher?"

"Friedman, think for a moment. Isn't Hawaii ridiculously far for McGovern to be going to collect his stupid recipes?"

"He's not only not Jewish, he's also not practical. I don't know which is worse."

"You've got to get out of that loft. Don't you have any other friends?"

"Imus is in New Mexico working on his cancer ranch for kids. Joel

Siegel's married with a small child. Mick Brennan's out of town on a photo shoot. Even Winnie Katz is busy from the sound of it. All my other friends are dead."

"They probably just got tired of listening to you talk about yourself."

"Just like I'm getting tired of watching this cat lick her vagina."

I heard what sounded very much like a telephone being hung up in Nassau. Sure enough, the blower was deader than a divorced dentist's Demerol-addicted dreams. Stephanie was like that, however. She was very young and she had a lot to learn. I was very middle-aged and I had a lot to learn. Like how to operate a childhood lighter.

"Good work," I said to the cat. "You've just torpedoed one of the most important relationships in my life."

The cat climbed up onto the desk, sat down precisely equidistant between the two red telephones, and looked at me. I don't usually believe in all that anthropomorphic tissue of horseshit like birds crying, dogs laughing, or people forgiving, but I could've sworn the cat was smiling.

Chapter Three

Everybody's alone in this world, though few of us realize it. Fewer still know how to appreciate the situation. Being alone gives you the opportunity to think, to dream, and to be yourself. You won't get that anywhere else. Do you really want to be part of a large Catholic family starving to death in some Third World country? Do you want to dine at a crowded, deadly dull Rotarian convention? See the world with an ethnocentric unwieldy group of German and Japanese tourists? Whine to your shrink about how you'd like to fucking kill yourself if you only had the balls?

While these are all admittedly attractive possibilities, why not enjoy the brief moments you have alone with yourself? They won't last long. Sooner or later some terrorist will drop by to give you a severed finger in a mayonnaise jar, or you'll suddenly find a stranger, who's just run out of hobbies, croaked on your dump machine.

When people know that you're alone they even find ways to screw up your loneliness. In the same fashion, if they're aware that you'll soon be leaving it's almost like you've already gone. People will be there for you if you don't want them, and if you really need them, they'll make themselves scarce. People'll never let you down. And don't let them tell you they've gotten any more sensitive or any cooler with the passage of time. The bullfighters and butterfly collectors are still among us, busily torturing and murdering Ferdinand the Friendly Bull and pinning up to pasteboards the tiny tattered wings of a million little Jesuses in the time it takes to sip a hot bitter cup of espresso.

That's pretty much what I was doing that cold morning in late January, sipping a cup of espresso. My whole life had come down to sipping a cup of espresso, puffing on the religious relic of an old Cuban cigar, and listening to the muted thuds of the lively little lesbian feet in the dance studio above my head. Things were not too bad yet, I reflected. You didn't really have a problem until you started thinking the lesbians were trying to send messages to you.

The espresso machine was humming. The city outside the loft was humming. My mind was humming, but it was a sweet old sad song from days gone by. I don't know what song the city was humming, but the espresso machine seemed to be working on a rather poignant version of "Hi Lili Hi Lo." The cat was asleep under her heat lamp on the desk. If I thought back I could remember periods of great excitement. Times when many things were happening to me both personally and professionally. But now, on this relentlessly gray morning of the first month of the new year, in a city turning older by the minute, there was absolutely nothing going on in my life. It was almost enough to make you believe in astrology.

I had changed from my old Borneo sarong and Robert Louis Stevenson purple bathrobe into jeans and a decrepit "Butt-Holdsworth Memorial Library" sweatshirt, had sorted through the detritus that was my mail, and was just thinking of making a nonstop trip to the dumper when the two red telephones on my desk rang in tandem. That was how they always rang, of course. They were, like every spinning ghost in the universe, connected to the same line. I hoisted the blower on the left.

"Start talkin'," I said.

"Aloha!" said a fond, familiar voice. "I think we may have a little problem."

The voice belonged to my old friend, the former beekeeper, Willis Hoover. Hoover currently was a columnist for the *Honolulu Advertiser,* and a dim recollection now came to me that he also currently had the misfortune of having McGovern as his housepest in Hawaii.

"Let me guess," I said. "McGovern got drunk and tried to hose Cari?" Cari was Hoover's girlfriend who worked in the Hawaiian prison system specializing in anger management.

"No such luck," said Hoover.

"McGovern got drunk and tried to hose you?"

"No such luck."

"Jesus," I said, "what did he do? Masturbate at the Pearl Harbor Memorial?"

"No such luck," said Hoover. "Let me take it from the top."

With a slight shudder I fired up a fresh cigar and settled back to hear Hoover's journalistic account of McGovern's adventures as his housepest. McGovern's exploits were the stuff of legend, so it would require quite a tawdry tale to surprise me. Nonetheless, I did feel a slight elbow in the colon at the note of concern I detected in Hoover's ever-fatalistic voice.

"We were out walking last night in Waikiki and I was showing McGovern the statue of Duke Kahanamoku, the father of modern surfing. The statue's about ten feet tall and the plaque says 'Actual Size,' but it's really only referring to the Duke's surfboard, which was sixteen feet long. Most tourists never knew who the Duke was, so I kept writing columns about the Duke and his statue, and eventually they put up another plaque identifying him so tourists wouldn't think he was the Jolly Green Giant or Darth Vader or somebody. Anyway, the last time I laid eyes on McGovern it was about midnight and he was just standing there staring at that statue."

"You mean he pulled his patented Mike McGovern disappearing act?"

"I remember thinking, 'Jesus, that fucker's almost as tall as the Duke's surfboard.' Then my attention must've wandered for a few moments and when I looked again he was gone."

"That's one of the most maddening things about McGovern," I said. "He's the largest person I know and he wanders off like a little child. He's done it a million times. He always comes back."

"Well, there's more," said Hoover. "I did a little detective work and followed his footprints down to the beach, which wasn't hard because they're about as big as the Duke's surfboard, too. They came to a certain point near the ocean and they just disappeared. All that was there was a notebook of his. Some recipe book he was working on apparently."

"Eat, Drink, and Be Kinky?"

"How'd you know that, Kinkyhead?"

"It's my business to know these things, Hoover."

"Well, all I'm saying is I'm worried about the boy. I've never lost a housepest yet and I don't want to start now. He hasn't shown up and he hasn't called."

"Relax, Hoover. He'll surface just when you least expect him."

"That's fine," said Hoover. "As long as he doesn't surface in the middle of the Pacific Ocean."

Chapter Four

You can't waste your time worrying too much about childlike creatures like McGovern. They go where they want to go and do what they want to do. McGovern once brushed his hair before meeting a racehorse. One time he met a Japanese tourist on the streets of New York and the guy asked him how to find the World Trade Center. "You found Pearl Harbor, didn't you?" McGovern told him. McGovern was unpredictable, mercurial, stubborn, curious, intelligent, kind, and well-traveled, yet oddly innocent of the ways of the world. It made for a rather tedious, troubling combination of traits, yet he always seemed to find his way home. Maybe God watched over people like McGovern.

I didn't give the whole matter of his disappearance too much thought that day as the afternoon turned colder and grayer than the morning, and the neolithic New York night lay waiting for its prey. Like Mark Twain, with a tinge of sadness, I felt that Hawaii was a place in my heart. In 1865 Twain had traveled to Hawaii as a young reporter, toured the islands, and in Honolulu met many people, millions of cats, and one king. He was the only reigning monarch Twain would ever see in his life, and some historians say it formed the basis for his later masterpiece, *A Connecticut Yankee in King Arthur's Court*.

As much as Twain truly loved Hawaii, thought about her, and dreamed about her, he was never to return. He sailed there in 1895, almost thirty years later, but because of a cholera epidemic in Honolulu, he was not allowed to go ashore. On a winter's day in New York, I suspect the Hawaii of the mind appears very similar to the one Twain looked at longingly from the rail of a distant ship at sea.

That afternoon and night passed in pretty much of a dull blur, with many medicinal shots of Jameson Irish Whiskey from the old bull's horn possibly not helping much in the rational thought department. I was still fairly confident that McGovern would turn up, probably with a colorful, humorous anecdote or two to add to his pantheon of puerile behavior. But there was something about the big man's disappearing so close to the edge of the beach that caused me to toss and turn that night like the restless waves of an endless ocean.

Around Faron Young Time, which had been designated as four o'clock in the morning by Dwight Yoakam and myself after the title of one of the late country singer's hit songs, I called Hoover again. Of course it was not Faron Young Time in Hawaii. It wasn't even Cinderella Time yet. But there'd been enough time for me to become more than a little concerned about the walking enigma that was McGovern. He was highly unpredictable, yet he always came through in the end. In other words, you couldn't set your watch by him, but you could, with at least some degree of accuracy, set your sundial or possibly even a rather slow hourglass. He was almost never there when you wanted him, but he was always there when you needed him. And, maybe most important, he was that rare human being who was actually considerate of other people's feelings. So it was that trait that gave me pause. Even if he'd drunk every little umbrella drink in Waikiki that night, he would've managed to slur some soothing message to his unfortunate host. But the usual drunken phone call from McGovern to Hoover had not yet occurred, at least not to my knowledge, and it'd now been almost forty-eight hours since the large man had gotten himself inexplicably lost in paradise.

"Greetings from the top of the food chain," said Hoover almost cheerfully once I'd raised him on the blower.

"So you've heard from McGovern?"

"Hell, no. I've just been thinking it over and I'm not as worried as I was the other night. I mean, it's weird behavior, but you know the guy a lot better than I do. He could be on Maui bodysurfing or something."

"To effectively bodysurf, McGovern would require a tsunami."

"That's true," Hoover said with a chuckle. He was the only living adult male I knew who actually could be said to chuckle. Women never chuckle. Children never chuckle. The great preponderance of men on this planet never chuckle. For one thing, there's damn little to chuckle about. It could possibly have something to do with Hoover's Iowa upbringing, I thought. I wasn't sure how sensitive Hoover was about his chuckle, however, and this didn't really seem the time or circumstance to go into it.

"He wasn't depressed or unhappy?" I asked. "He didn't say anything before he disappeared?"

"Let me think. Wait a minute. He did seem rather distracted, as I recall. The last thing I remember him saying was, 'I'd like to take some horizontal hula lessons from that dame coming out of Denny's by the Sea.'"

"'I'd like to take some horizontal hula lessons from that dame coming out of Denny's by the Sea'?"

"Those were his last spoken words. Then her boyfriend came out. He was a big Samoan. Even bigger than McGovern—"

"That's not possible."

"Then he went over to the statue of the Duke. You know, the more I think about it, he's probably shacking up in some hotel room near the beach. Maybe he decided to go island-hopping and just didn't realize his gracious host might be worried. Maybe he lost my number."

"Maybe you're in denial," I said.

"That's very possible," said Hoover. "I've been in denial most of my life."

Before cradling the blower I extracted from Hoover a promise that were there any phone calls or two-legged whale sightings or any information at all concerning the whereabouts of one Michael R. McGovern, he would contact me immediately. In a somewhat ambivalent state I wandered over to the espresso machine, opened diplomatic relations, and listened to that shiny steel dingus that took up approximately a third of my little kitchen hum a rather Anglicized version of "Aloha Oe," the haunting farewell song the last Hawaiian monarch, Queen Liliuokalani, wrote in prison. That was how I watched the dawn's surly light insinuate itself into the loft and the world, listening to a highly empathetic espresso machine, sporadically sipping the

31

comforting nectar that flowed thereof, puffing a recently resurrected cigar, and wondering what the hell was going to happen next.

It didn't take long to find out. At a quarter after seven both red blowers went off like the fire alarm in Zelda Fitzgerald's sanitarium. I hastily hoisted the blower on the left but it was not Hoover. It was a sobbing Stephanie calling from Nassau. Her sixteen-year-old Maltese, Pyramus, who'd been staying with friends in New York while she was away, had died in its sleep last night.

I tried to say all the right things like, "Peace be with her," and, "She had a wonderful life," and, "She died peacefully," and, "I, like every other man on the planet, envied her closeness to you," but at a time like that very little is likely to take. She had made plans to return to New York that afternoon for "the funeral." I had never attended the funeral of a Maltese, I reflected, and I probably never would because I apparently wasn't invited to this one. Had I been, I don't know what I'd have done. It's always struck me as especially sad to see a strong, confident, beautiful woman that you think you love, collapse.

I walked over to the kitchen window and watched Vandam Street groggily waking up. I recalled the many times I'd stood there and witnessed Pyramus and Thisbe at Stephanie's stiletto heels marching obliviously in and out of my life. For some reason I thought of something Stephanie had once told me. She'd said that whenever you see a sign at a hotel or motel that says "No Pets Allowed," it really means "No Friends Allowed." I kept looking at the street but I wasn't seeing anything. It felt like someone had poured cinnamon oil in my eyes.

"The world's a sadder and a colder place this morning," I said to the cat. "A little friend of ours has died and a big friend is missing."

The cat, of course, said nothing. She appeared to be obsessed with a cockroach currently crawling along the windowsill.

I said nothing more, for I'd learned a long time ago never to question the grief of others. It is quite enough to question the grief within yourself.

Chapter Five

The death of Pyramus, tiny little creature that she was, cast a giant pall over 199B Vandam Street. Even before the return from Nassau of that grieving goddess Stephanie DuPont, the mood inside the loft and the interpersonal relations between man and cat seemed surprisingly subdued. It is true that the cat bore no special fondness for Stephanie's *enfants,* yet it was clear that she recognized through many millennia of feline cultural sensitivity that our little world had been, in some immutable way, significantly diminished.

As for myself, I recognized through many millennia of cumbersome human bumbling the mortality of all God's creatures great and small. If one as little and harmless and innocent as Pyramus could perish, I reasoned, so very possibly could one as large and harmless and innocent as McGovern. Everything was interwoven in this best of all possible worlds, like a cheap sweater made by child labor in Pakistan. By the late afternoon, I was in what Billy Joe Shaver called a "slow-rollin' low." I wasn't exactly sure where Pyramus ended or McGovern began, or if, indeed, it was the other way around.

"We can no longer help poor Pyramus," I remarked to the cat later that evening. "But there must be something we can do to help McGovern. Unless, of course, he's bodysurfing on Maui."

The cat appeared to reflect very briefly upon the subject, then closed her eyes and went back to sleep on her favorite rocking chair. It was, indeed, the only rocking chair in the loft. It was not, however, the only chair. My eyes gazed across the room to the large, overstuffed chair McGovern himself had given me. Rambam had commented later that accepting a hand-me-down from McGovern might not be best foot forward for my image. Now I thought of the last time McGovern had visited the loft and I remembered him sitting down in that very chair. It was an old chair and his large torso sank into it a good bit further than he'd apparently expected, resulting in his sitting about six inches from the floor and giving the decidedly rather comical appearance of the chair having swallowed McGovern.

"Local man disappears in chair," McGovern had commented at the time.

The chair was empty now, of course, much like the feeling in my heart. More than forty-eight hours had elapsed since McGovern had disappeared. By NYPD standards my favorite Irish poet was now officially a missing person. Or were the cops supposed to wait seventy-two hours? I wasn't sure. I'd have to check with Rambam. But Rambam, practically speaking, was a missing person himself at the moment. He was in Israel trying on a yarmulke or having sex with a camel, which was about as helpful to McGovern at the moment as a man in New York smoking a cigar, sipping an espresso, and talking to a cat.

"It's time to go to the authorities," I said to the cat, "but *which* authorities?"

The cat remained silent but cast a quick, green, doubtful glance in my direction. She had always questioned authority. It was the way of her people.

"Hawaii's a little outside of Sergeant Cooperman's or Sergeant Fox's bailiwick. Maybe we should call Jack Lord."

The cat, of course, said nothing.

"You remember Jack Lord," I implored the now peacefully slumbering feline. "*Hawaii Five-O*! Book 'em, Danno!"

I was now pacing frenetically up and down the chilly living room of the loft, my nervous, schizophrenian, Sherlockian energy almost in perfect spiritual counterpoint to the cat's serene, somnolent, not to say slothful, state of rest. I was puffing on my cigar like the train that plunged over the bridge on the River Kwai, getting more excited now, almost oblivious to the music and the thudding from Winnie's dance studio that had now started up directly over my head.

Strictly in terms of mental hygiene, what I saw before me was not a pretty scene: the flames from the fireplace painting the loft in a livid, devilish glare. The little black puppet head smiling sickly down upon me from the mantel. The Terpsichorean Sisters of Sappho above now reprising a number I hadn't heard them performing in years. Could it be? Yes, it could. "Gonna Wash That Man Right Out of My Hair." I'd visited Nurse's Beach in Kauai along with Miss Texas 1987, the precise location where the song and dance number was filmed in the movie version of *South Pacific*. The nurses were all gone now, of course. Time and Richard Speck had done their work, I suppose. Miss Texas 1987 was gone, too. In fact, almost everything was gone from my life now except the smoke from my cigar mingling with the smoke from the little fireplace mingling with the shadows and the sunlight in my mind. Life is tragedy, I thought. Love is war, I thought. All colors fade, I thought.

"You know, I remember reading some time ago in my *National Enquirer*," I said to the cat, "that Jack Lord was either dead or suffering from Alzheimer's, I can't remember which. Maybe everybody in the world's either dead or suffering from Alzheimer's and none of us can remember which."

I turned to see if the cat was at least awake, but, of course, she wasn't. Her loss, I figured.

"The point is, when someone goes missing in a place like Hawaii you don't get worried as quickly as if they turned up missing in some more dangerous place like Afghanistan or Guatemala or Florida. For all we know McGovern's large, sunburned body may be lying on Nurse's Beach at this very moment, very possibly on top of a nurse. Hell, he could be anywhere along that gorgeous chain of tropical islands that all began when a volcano erupted, the lava cooled, and a passing bird took a lucky flying dump that contained within it a tiny seed that started the whole fucking thing. At least that's what scientists believe. Of course, they've never been right yet."

When I ended my harangue and looked across the room I found that the cat was no longer in the rocker. Whether it was a show of solidarity, a casual circumstance, or a singularly ill omen, I did not know, but the cat was now watching me intensely from the vantage point of McGovern's old chair.

Chapter Six

"**Why do pets** have to conk?" wailed Stephanie over the blower the following morning.

I didn't really have an answer and fortunately one wasn't required. Before I could take my first cigar of the morning out of my mouth, she was on again with what was essentially the oddly poignant eulogy of a little girl growing up too fast in a world gone suddenly sad.

"Pyramus was such a sweet, loving pet and she never harmed a soul and all her life all she wanted was to be with me and she died while I was away—"

"Yes, but she did die peacefully in her sleep."

"I know, but the apartment's so *empty* without her. Baby Savannah keeps looking around everywhere for her—"

"Then you're back in town."

"No, Dickhead, I'm calling you from the South Pole."

"Well, I'm really sorry about poor little Pyramus. As my father says at times like this, 'She's now in the hands of a higher authority.'"

"Why do pets have to conk?"

"I don't know, darling. As my sister says, 'There are no bad dogs; there are no good people.'"

"Stop quoting everybody in your fucking family."

"I have a small, ill-tempered family and I'm rather fond of quoting them."

"That's probably why all your friends left town. They were sick of you quoting your family all the time. Don't you have any original thoughts that aren't about yourself?"

"Well, I'm not a fucking Hallmark card, but let me think. How about this? 'As you walk through life, you'll hold her leash more than you know.'"

"That's pretty cornball. Maybe you are a fucking Hallmark card. The funeral's this afternoon, by the way. I'm burying Pyramus in a little garden. A very private affair. You and your sick cat are not invited."

"Too bad. I kind of enjoy funerals. They have an inherent honesty that most weddings seem to lack."

"I enjoy funerals, too. Especially if they happen to be yours."

I started to say something, but I soon realized that the blower, like the subject matter under discussion, not to mention the relationship itself, had gone dead in my hand. I set it down gently in its cradle with the soft finality that might come to you if you were burying a small dog. Grieving women had never been my long suit anyway. At the moment I wasn't sure what my long suit was. Maybe it was still at the cleaners.

Just in case you're wondering what the death of a small dog has to do with the apparent disappearance of a large friend, the answer, very possibly, is not a hell of a lot. There is, however, a good bit of cosmic linkage between the two events, and when a light rain began falling later in the afternoon I sort of wished the cat and I had been invited to Pyramus's funeral if only to hold an umbrella over Stephanie's broken heart. But there seemed to be a seepage of sadness connecting the hot tears on Stephanie's face for her little pet to the woeful waves of the Pacific Ocean lapping that distant tropical shore where McGovern had vanished from the face of the earth. The combination of the two disasters had unleashed an impotent rage emanating from my heart and directed squarely at the universe in general.

"We must put the Pyramus matter to rest," I said to the cat. "She's sheltered and safe from sorrow. As for McGovern, he always turns up sooner or later, wagging his tail behind him. We are, however, a significant part of the only family he has. If he is in some kind of trouble and I don't act now, I could never forgive myself if he came to grief."

The cat sat on the kitchen counter looking at me doubtfully. In her narrow experience there were no faraway places and everyone who went away always came back.

I was just winding up my little lecture to the cat when both red telephones on my desk took off for Venus. I moved with all possible haste in that direction.

"That'll be Hoover," I said, as I picked up the blower on the left. But it wasn't. It was Rambam.

"Perfect timing," I said.

"Don't tell me you're hosin' again."

"No such luck. But I do need your expert consultation on a certain problem that has arisen. Where are you, Rambam?"

"I'm in a little town called Umm-al-Fakem calling you on my shoe phone."

"What're you doing there?"

"Watching Arabs throw rocks. What's the problem?"

"McGovern's disappeared on a beach in Hawaii."

"Has he *really* disappeared or just wandered off again?"

"That's the problem. I've known him to pull this when traveling with me in Australia, Tahiti, Mexico, San Antonio, and the East Village to name a few memorable locations. He *is* one-half American Indian, you know. You can't blame him for unconsciously straying off the reservation now and then. And the other half's Irish, of course, so you can't blame him for not promptly coming back. But it's been three days now and—"

"Three days!" shouted Rambam. "Three fuckin' days! What if he's really missing? What if he's been abducted—"

"That's ridiculous. No one on the planet would want to kidnap McGovern. For one thing, he doesn't know anyone with the bucks to pay the ransom. For another, he's too large to abduct. Foul play is out of the question."

"That's exactly where you're wrong, Kinky. Never assume what might've happened to a missing person. This is not just about kids on fucking milk cartons. The first twenty-four hours are absolutely crucial. After that the tide washes away things that could be clues. Tourists leave who might've been eyewitnesses. Look, where was McGovern staying in Hawaii?"

"In Honolulu with my friend Hoover—"

"Have Hoover call 911 *now*. Have them scan the beaches, check the hospitals, check the morgue. If Hoover and the cops don't turn up something, the next step is for you to fly out there with a current photo of McGovern to slap on every telephone pole and surfboard in sight. If you don't turn up something, the next step is really unpleasant, because it means I have to fly my ass out there and if I have to go halfway around the world to locate McGovern he better at least be a fucking amnesia victim. I don't want to find him wearing a funny straw hat, drinking mai tais, and playing beach blanket bingo with a bevy of rejects from *Baywatch*."

"Which is still the most likely scenario in my opinion."

"You may very well be right," said Rambam, "but you've got to cover all the bases if you want to be a good little private investigator . . . Jesus Christ!!!"

"What was that?"

"A rock."

"Are you okay?"

"I'm fine. It's not my car."

"Great. Whose is it?"

"Hertz Rent-a-Car of Bethlehem."

"Perfect. Look, I got to go. I've got to call Hoover."

"Okay, but listen. Don't get all bent out of shape about this. It's all just routine missing persons investigative procedure. When you've searched high and low it'll probably turn out to be the *Baywatch* situation."

"I'll keep that in mind."

"By the way," said Rambam cheerfully, "is McGovern a virgin?"

"Not since he was thirteen. Why do you ask?"

"Because they might've thrown him into the volcano."

Chapter Seven

Hoover, having once been a beekeeper, was a highly industrious person. It would not take him long, I figured, to grasp the basic Rambam routine missing persons investigative procedure, set his ears back, and run with it. I needed Hoover to be my man on the ground in Hawaii. To start the whole megillah into motion you only had to punch three numbers on a telephone, but even that couldn't be done from New York. I also needed Hoover to very promptly snap out of a lifetime of denial, which was not, of course, limited to Hoover but extended to practically every deluded, misguided soul on this ship of fools we call planet earth.

"What if he just lost my phone number?" Hoover wanted to know once I'd raised him on the blower.

"We can't take that chance," I said.

"What if he just went on a three-day bender?"

"We can't take that chance," I said.

By the time I cradled the blower both Hoover and myself were in no mood to be taking any chances. If McGovern was anywhere on that magical chain of islands, we damn well intended to find him. Hoover reminded me that all things, including missing persons investigations, moved slowly in Hawaii, and I reminded him that time was precious now, he might have to take a personal hand with things like visiting the hospitals, checking the morgue, making sure the cops stayed on the case.

"It'll be easy," he'd told me before he'd rung off. "It's what I do anyway. It's a reporter's life."

"A reporter's life," I'd told him, "is exactly what may hang in the balance."

For the first time since McGovern had disappeared I felt a wave of relief wash through the ragged atmosphere of the loft. A practical, cohesive plan was now in place to get to the bottom of this troublesome and disturbing affair. Even in the eyes of the cat I seemed to notice a rare gleam of what looked very much like mild approval for my actions. Either that or it was time for me to check into Zelda Fitzgerald's sanitarium.

That evening I bundled up against the cold and trundled on down to Chinatown, after first removing three cigars for the road from Sherlock Holmes's porcelain head. His gray lonely eyes seemed to flash in the firelight, or was it gaslight, as I ankled it out of the loft, a singular sign of mild approval on his part as well. I was so taken by this unexpected gesture that I almost left him in charge of the loft. My better angels carried the moment, however, as I realized that such an intemperate move would undoubtedly send the cat into a highly unpleasant, petulant snit for days to come. So I left the cat in charge and got the hell out of there.

I hailed a hack on Hudson and headed down to Canal where I bailed out about six blocks before Mott Street in order to take in the ambience of the living street. I hadn't been out of the loft since Christ was a cowboy. It wasn't a bad thing to get out occasionally and see people who reminded you of other people who reminded you that no man was an island, with the possible exception of McGovern, who was almost large and dense enough to be one and it was hoped wasn't floating right now somewhere out in the middle of the Pacific Ocean.

Was I worried about McGovern? You bet I was. Was I angry with McGovern? You bet I was. Almost as angry as I was with myself for not being able to keep pets from conking or friends and lovers and loved ones from disappearing from my life. I should've put up a sign at the entrance to my loft that read "No Friends Allowed." Maybe they'd wise up and stay away. At least if McGovern was dead I wasn't going to have to tell his family. Just the man in the mirror. That was it. Just the guy in the cowboy hat and the coat made from an Indian blanket who was smoking a cigar and staring down his weary reflection in the window of a cheap Chinese coffee shop. The guy in the window wanted McGovern to be alive. The guy in the window wanted pets to never have to conk. The name of the restaurant was Fuk Yu.

I dined alone that night at Big Wong's sitting across the table from an extremely old Chinese man with an extremely long white hair growing out of a mole on his withered cheek. As the old guy slurped his pork gruel I remember thinking, "That's me in six months." I walked all the way back to Vandam through the cold emptiness of the crowded night streets. A man and wife were dancing inside my head. Then they started to argue.

"Hop the next plane to Honolulu," said the man. "That's crazy," said the woman. "At least wait till you hear from Hoover." By the time I got to the loft the guy had gone out for cigarettes.

Chapter Eight

It's not often when the cat and I get visitors to our humble loft, but when we do we assiduously endeavor to make the visit a memorable experience for our guests. Later that night three of them—Stephanie, Thisbe, and Baby Savannah—blessed our loft with their presence and the result was a very unpleasant situation. I will blithely skip over the initial ugliness and bring you right to where things stood at the moment.

Stephanie, for example, stood over six feet tall in her blood-red stilettoes, and was contenting herself by berating me on two fronts simultaneously: why I hadn't told her earlier about McGovern's disappearance, and why I didn't have a certain French wine in the apartment.

Thisbe and Baby Savannah were bouncing off the walls and impersonating whirling dervishes back and forth across the length of the loft. The cat, hanging onto the inside of the closed bedroom door where I'd had to put her, was emitting a loud, ululating, vaguely Palestinian keening sound that penetrated the entire building and I hoped was causing some mild irritation as well to the lesbian dance class.

"I don't drink French wine," I said, as calmly as possible under the circumstances. "I pour it out on the sidewalk to protest their nuclear testing in the South Pacific."

"Which is where poor McGovern is right now."

"Not quite," I said. "If I went out looking for McGovern in the

South Pacific I'd never find him. It's a rather common misnomer that Hawaii's in the South Pacific. Actually, it's in the southernmost part of the North Pacific."

"How fascinating! It's so wonderful for a young girl to be able to learn these kinds of things from such an older, more experienced man. How long's he been missing, Dickhead?"

"About three days now, but Hoover's—"

"Three days!!" shouted Stephanie, as Baby Savannah bounced heavily against my scrotum like a cannonball covered with white fluff. "Three fucking days!! Oh, Friedman, why didn't you *tell* me that?"

"I didn't want to upset you before the funeral—"

"There's going to be *another* funeral if you don't get that sick cat to shut up!"

"Darling, I think it's fair to say that the cat's just upset about Thisbe's rather high-pitched, though certainly not unpleasant, barking and Baby Savannah's bouncing cheerfully all over the place like a hyperactive Ping-Pong ball."

"Your brain's like a hyperactive Ping-Pong ball. Don't you *realize*, Inspector Parakeet Dick, that by this time McGovern's either *dead*—"

From the direction of the bedroom came a sudden shriek so blood-curdling that it caused Stephanie's beautiful face to pale almost precisely to the shade of the porcelain countenance of the nearby bust of Sherlock Holmes. I don't know what my face looked like, but I only had to look at it in the windows of Chinese restaurants, so it wasn't my problem. I did notice that Baby Savannah, who'd been sniffing around under the bedroom door, was now performing a rather peculiar little ice-picking yelp and bounding rapidly back toward Stephanie with a scratch on her cute, inquisitive little nose.

"Poor darling," said Stephanie, taking Baby into her arms. "Did that sick cat hurt your precious little nose?"

"It doesn't look too serious," I said in a reassuring tone.

"Of course it's not *serious*. It didn't happen to *you*. Everything's okay, darling. Mommy's taking care of you. Don't just stand there, Friedman! Get a warm washcloth! A *clean* warm washcloth."

Getting a clean warm washcloth, in fact finding any kind of washcloth at all in the loft, was going to be only a little bit harder than locating a bottle of French wine. The last time I'd come into contact with a washcloth had been several years ago, brought to me afterward by a person I suspected of being a terrorist and a woman, but as of this writing cannot vouch for either as a certainty. The incident was probably best described by McGovern who remarked later: "A blow job given with love is as beautiful as dogs playing poker."

Baby Savannah most definitely didn't look like the kind of dog you'd ever see playing poker. Maybe she'd enter the Pebble Beach backgammon tournament or play miniature croquet. But the scratch was very minor and what the hell was I doing wandering around in the rain room pretending to be looking for a clean, warm washcloth that I knew wasn't there when my dear old friend McGovern might, at this very moment, be wandering around lost in some tropical jungle, the victim of amnesia?

What I was at last able to find was an extralarge beach towel that, because it was a dark purple, didn't look dirty and therefore never needed to be washed. I took it over to the sink and dutifully ran some hot water onto it, then, as I waited for the towel to cool slightly, I glanced up to see if the Gypsy in the bathroom mirror was in. He wasn't, and hadn't been for quite a while. As I studied that silver plane that gently reminds us of time passing and sadness in our eyes and, once in a while, points out to the alert observer the unfortunate presence of a six-inch-long nose hair, I could hear Stephanie shouting from the kitchen: "Hurry up, Friedman! She may go into shock." As I departed the dumper I noticed that the waving fields of grain I'd once imagined in the mirror now appeared to be ruthless, fractious waves in an amoral, infinite ocean. Was the Gypsy trying to tell me that McGovern was dead? Was McGovern trying to tell me that he was alive? And what had Stephanie been trying to tell me just before this bit of unpleasantness had erupted?

"Mommy will take care of you, darling," said Stephanie, as I came out of the rain room. "Uncle Kinky and his sick cat didn't mean to hurt you."

"It's all I could find," I said, as I handed her the large purple beach towel.

"What's that?" she said. "A washcloth that wants to take over the world?"

"How's Baby?"

"She'll live. Which is more than I can say for your cat if she *ever* touches Baby again. Everything's fine, darling. Mommy didn't mean to raise her voice."

I walked over to a small cabinet and took out a bottle of Gammel Dansk, the powerful, slightly hallucinogenic drink that can make you stray rather dangerously off the reservation. I poured a hefty shot into the old bull's horn and another into a viking-horn shot glass a friend from Sweden had sent me. I took a glass in each hand and walked over to the counter where Stephanie was almost finished administering to Baby Savannah. I put the drink in her hand and clinked those two odd receptacles together in a toast.

"*Slainte,*" I said, which is pronounced "sa-*lan*'-cha" for those who can't read Gaelic.

"What is it?" asked Stephanie, not injudiciously.

"The drink is Danish," I said. "The toast is Irish."

"Why can't you just say *l'chaim* like a normal Hebe?"

"Because if I were a normal Hebe—indeed, if I were a normal person—the roots of my manhood would not run deep enough into my soul in order to enable me to survive the withering amount of bullshit that I joyously receive on a fairly regular basis from the smartest, most beautiful, and wittiest twenty-four-year-old woman in the world whom I gladly would die for."

"Never end a sentence with a preposition," she said.

We drank the Gammel Dansk together. It went down my throat like a high-speed bobsled and I could see Stephanie was having the same experience with the bitter brew. Moments later, however, it had the pleasant effect of mildly disorienting both of us.

"Now what were you saying about McGovern just before the cat began ululating like a Palestinian woman?"

"That he's the only friend of yours I like?"

"No. You were saying that after being missing for three days he was either *dead*—"

"Dead. Yes, it's possible."

"But you said *either* dead. Either dead or *what?*"

"Or he's like my heart sometimes," said Stephanie in the voice of a small child half-whispering half-forgotten words. "He doesn't want to be found."

Chapter Nine

Stephanie, Thisbe, and the much-fussed-over Baby Savannah had barely departed the loft, and the cat had just driven out of the bedroom in a 1937 Monstro-snit, when the phones rang. I was busy pouring myself a Gammel Dansk nightcap to settle me down from all the stress, so I quickly killed the shot, swallowed the bitter bobsled, and legged it over to the desk.

"That'll be Hoover," I said to the cat.

The cat, of course, said nothing. Indeed, it was highly problematic whether she would ever speak to me again. I picked up the blower on the left.

"Tampons are us," I said.

"Kinky, this is F. Murray Abraham" said the voice. "I'm looking for McGovern."

"Who isn't?" I said.

I'd met and got to know Murray on my second voyage aboard the *QE2*. I was performing country music and Murray, "You can call me F.," was the guest lecturer on the subject of what it was like to star in two ridiculously disparate hit movies at precisely the same time, *Amadeus* and *Scarface*. On my first crossing aboard the *QE2*, accompanied by the former Miss Texas 1987, I met and hung out with Robert Stack, whom I found to be a great and humorous American. I was understandably somewhat reticent to ever take a third trip aboard the *QE2*. There was always the possibility that I might have to meet and get to know myself.

"McGovern has asked me to contribute a recipe for his new book," Abraham was saying. *"Eat, Drink, and Be Kinky."*

"Great title," I said distractedly.

"So I've meticulously assembled a salad recipe along with a terrific liquor concoction and now I've tried to call him repeatedly—"

"It doesn't look like there's going to be a recipe book," I said. "McGovern's disappeared in Hawaii."

"How'd it happen? When did it happen?"

"All I know is he vanished from the beach at Waikiki about three nights ago and no one's seen or heard from him since."

"That's bad. If he drowned, how long would it take for the tide to wash his body back on shore?"

"How many crossties on a railroad, Murray? How many stars in the sky? How the hell do I know? You'd think that a guy who rides a bicycle around New York City, is the only tenant in his building who steadfastly refuses to go co-op, and lets the guy who runs the corner pizza place handle his tax returns, would have enough good sense not to get himself drowned in Hawaii."

"I'm not sure that follows. But this is terrible news. What are you going to do?"

"What can I do? We're checking all the beaches and hospitals and hotels and the morgue. If he doesn't turn up pretty damn quick I'm hopping a plane out there myself and slapping posters of McGovern everywhere. I don't know what else to do—"

"I don't know if that poster thing will work. People get an idea in their heads and they can't see what's right in front of their eyes. They're always coming up to me, for instance, and telling me how great I was in *Gandhi.* But I wasn't in *Gandhi.* That was Ben Kingsley. I've even signed autographs 'F. Ben Kingsley' because the people don't believe me."

"Well, I've got to do something soon. I can't just sit here and swap recipes. What do you know about amnesia, Murray?"

"Not much," said Abraham. "Ben Kingsley hasn't done any amnesia movies."

Half an hour later, after I'd donned my old purple Robert Louis Stevenson bathrobe, fed the cat some moist and tender gourmet sliced chicken, which she pointedly ignored, and got out my JFK pipe for a long night of sleeplessness, the phones rang. I said, "That'll be Hoover," and it was. Unfortunately, he didn't have a lot of light to shed on what was turning into an increasingly sorry situation. Everything was being done that could be done. No trace of McGovern had been found.

"The good news," said Hoover, "if there is any, is that his body hasn't washed up on the beach yet. The bad news is that the cops just seem to be going through the motions. They quite literally don't have a clue."

"What if McGovern's wandering around right now with amnesia? Maybe when you weren't looking he tried to head-butt the Duke's surfboard. If he didn't drown, they ought to be able to find him."

"Not these cops. They sit in their squad cars drinking Kona coffee and eating *malasadas.* I've stayed on their case but it's hard to generate any sustained activity in a missing persons investigation in a tropical paradise."

"What about *Hawaii Five-O*? Isn't there some special unit like that? I mean, I read in my *National Enquirer* where Jack Lord had Alzheimer's—"

"That's great," Hoover chuckled darkly. "An Alzheimer's victim going out in search of an amnesia victim."

"Jack Lord might even be dead."

"That'd make it even harder for him to conduct the investigation. Why don't you just come out here? You found Willie Nelson when he was missing. Maybe you can find McGovern, too."

"Willie at least left me some clues."

"Maybe McGovern did, too. Why don't you get your ass out here, Kinkyhead?"

It was a good question and it deserved an answer. Better yet it deserved my immediate commitment if I was going to have any chance at all of finding my favorite Irish poet alive.

"A friend's got to do what a friend's got to do," I said to the cat, as I took out the brown leather suitcase Stephanie had, during happier times, ordered for me from a catalog using my credit card.

The cat thrashed her tail wildly and her eyes glinted yellow, then green. Obviously, she did not concur with my statement. Friendship, she felt, was an archaic, overrated sentiment. Friends were there to use you, she believed, to take advantage of you when you were doing well, and desert you when you were down. It was a dog-eat-dog world, and that was all right with the cat. I didn't necessarily disagree with her, never having done quite well enough to fully test her theory.

But cats are often quite private creatures when it comes to sharing their pains and fears and anxieties. It was entirely possible that her eminently negative reaction was not brought about by my statement of loyalty to my dear friend McGovern, but rather engendered by the unwelcome act of my taking out the suitcase. Most cats do not like to travel very far and are filled with disdain and disgust for those misguided souls who occasionally do. This attitude of the cat's, while rather provincial, was quite understandable. For the cat had never required a rearview mirror in which to see herself.

I had just tossed a few Hawaiian shirts and my old Peace Corps sarong into the suitcase when the phones rang again. I listened to them ring for a moment, imagining perhaps that the instruments had been imbued with a sentient quality, almost a sense of urgency. It was late, of course. It was one Gammel Dansk over the line. It could've been anyone. Could've even been a wrong number. But it wasn't.

"Start talkin'," I said, as I hefted the blower on the left.

It was a strange voice and a bad connection and it sounded like it was emanating from some faraway place like Lower Baboon's Asshole. But the words would be forever emblazoned upon my scrotum.

"Hang loose," said the voice. "Lono is home."

Before I could respond, I heard another voice, dearly familiar, yet urgent-sounding and even further away.

"MIT!—MIT!—MIT!" it said.

Then the line went dead.

PART TWO

On the Fly

Chapter Ten

The Gulfstream IV skipped like a silver stone high above the coast of California, winging its westward way to Hawaii. The private jet was compliments of my friend John McCall, the shampoo king from Dripping Springs, the little town outside of Austin where Willie Nelson had held his very first Fourth of July picnic. When Willie had voluntarily vanished in Hawaii several years back, John had chartered a private jet to help me find him. But we'd found Willie in just a matter of a little over three days. McGovern had already been missing for longer than that.

"I brought two books with me for the trip," said McCall from the seat across the narrow aisle. "One is this big thick volume called *Power,* written by some self-help business nerd. He says power is the key not only to success but also even to freedom and happiness, which is why everybody, whether consciously or unconsciously, spends his life pursuing power."

"He's right," I said.

"The other book I'm reading is *The Great Gatsby,*" said McCall, "in which Fitzgerald poignantly demonstrates that all power is merely illusion and has nothing whatsoever to do with ultimate success, not to mention freedom or happiness."

"He's right," I said.

"Wait a minute," said McCall. "The business nerd says power is everything and you say he's right. Fitzgerald says power is nothing and you say *he's* right. They can't *both* be right."

"You're right, too," I said.

But I wasn't really into the conversation. My thoughts were in Chicago where a single, middle-aged man had died in his apartment years ago. Everyone who knew him had assumed he wasn't home or else they didn't care or maybe his wonderful friends were all working on their projects and in a sense he was too if you consider his project to be having cats and rats eat his body while waiting to see how long it would take for anyone to notice he'd fallen through the trap door.

McGovern had caught the news story on the wire and read it to me and this had brought into being the Man-in-Trouble Hot Line by which each of us stayed in touch and frequently called the other party with the salutation "MIT—MIT—MIT!!" Quite often if one of us was bored, depressed, or in imminent danger of hanging himself by the heels from an espresso machine, the message could simply be left on the other party's answering machine and not long after, some semblance of human contact would be achieved.

The Man-in-Trouble Hot Line probably could've saved a lot of people, I reflected. Oscar Wilde could've called Emily Dickinson from a pay phone in the rain. Gauguin could've shared his restlessness on Tahiti with Robert Louis Stevenson's loneliness on Samoa. Davy Crockett from the Alamo could've left a message for Phil Hartman. Sylvia Plath might not have put her head in the oven. Ernest Hemingway might not have blown his brains into the orange juice. Richard Corey might not have gone home one night and put a bullet in his head. Sonny Liston could've called John Henry or Juliet or Jesus and the cops might not have found thirteen days' worth of newspapers on his front porch in Las Vegas. But the Man-in-Trouble Hot Line can't save everybody. There's no time between the windmill and the world to buy a Van Gogh, help Mozart out of the gutter, Sharansky out of the Gulag, Rosa out of the back of the bus, or Anne out of the attic. Funny what you think about on a plane.

"When you first told me two nights ago about the big guy disappearing," McCall was saying, "I put Russell Walker on the case. You know Russell. He's got contacts with the FBI, the DEA, even the CIA. All the initials. They're all looking for McGovern on Hawaii. If they can't find him, nobody can."

"I hope they find him, but I doubt it."

"Then who would you suggest we hire? The Canadian Mounted Police?"

"If you like initials, how about hiring MM?"

"What's MM?"

"Not what. Who."

"Okay, who's MM?" said McCall, showing the first slight signs of irritation.

"Miss Marple," I said.

McCall looked at me like I was an outpatient and turned over a page in one of his two books. I turned over in my mind the last phone call I'd received before I'd left New York. "Hang loose. Lono is home." And then, of course, a muffled-sounding, troubled-sounding, desperate-sounding McGovern muttering "MIT—MIT—MIT!!!"

"All we know," I said to McCall, "is the information contained in that phone call I got. We know McGovern was alive forty-eight hours ago. We know he's in trouble, possibly held captive by persons unknown. It would help if we knew who Lono was."

"Why don't you ask Miss Marple?"

I was pondering John's question when a little white ball of fluff bounded suddenly up my leg, catapulted off my scrotum onto my shoulder, and hopscotched onto the top of my head.

"Baby Savannah!" shouted a stern, shrill voice from somewhere behind me.

Baby and I carefully, instinctively, and simultaneously turned our heads to see a lovely, languid figure reclining comfortably on the couch with Thisbe and her bible, the current issue of *People*.

"Get down from Uncle Kinky's head, darling," said Stephanie. "You don't know where that head has been."

Chapter Eleven

Getting Stephanie to agree to accompany me on the trip had not been the easiest of propositions. To my mind there were three basic reasons why she went along. First, while she felt disgust for Ratso and distrust for Rambam, she genuinely liked McGovern and thought he was "sweet." If McGovern hadn't been missing and possibly in dire peril, I might've been jealous. The second reason Stephanie came, not sexually, was that little Pyramus's death had created a bleak, melancholy atmosphere for her in New York and a change of scene seemed definitely best foot forward under the sad circumstances. The third reason I believe she consented to go was that McCall's private jet would be able to whisk Baby Savannah and Thisbe right to the destination without quarantines, red tape, or danger or discomfort for the two tiny travelers.

Why John McCall agreed to charter a jet at very short notice and go with me to Hawaii was easy. I was his friend and McGovern was his friend and he liked to travel, blow bucks on crazy things, and go on wild goose chases as long as his own goose didn't get cooked in the process, and sometimes he didn't care about that.

Why I went to Hawaii was simple. I thought that I probably knew McGovern better than anybody else in the world. If the FBI, the CIA, and the DEA couldn't find him with all their manpower and resources, maybe I could with an intimate knowledge of his half–Native American, half-Irish, often half-marinated, brilliant mind. At the very least I could take some of the pressure off Hoover. It was really too much to ask the same human being to put up with McGovern as a housepest, then, just as you're recovering from that singularly repellent experience, be called upon to head up the investigation to find him again.

Finding a big guy like McGovern on a small island chain shouldn't be the hardest thing in the world. But there were places in Hawaii where haoles feared to tread. There were remote beaches filled with Vietnam vets locked in a deadly rictus of eternal flashback. There were secret underwater caves only ancient gnarled kahunas dared attempt entry. There were empty villages, desolated by leprosy, inhabited only by ghosts. There were places in Hawaii where rituals of blood and fire and human sacrifice were still redolent in the sweet and dangerous perfumed night air.

A sense of deep futility swam in tandem with a sense of dark foreboding down a synaptic nightmarish stream of thought I couldn't get out of my fevered brain. "Hang loose," said a voice in my head as I looked down upon the glittering, gaping, tragic Pacific. How can you hang loose when you're careening across a chasm of chaos to find a friend who can't be found? "Lono is home," said the voice. But who the hell was Lono and where was home and where was Lono before he was home? Just the facts, ma'am.

"Don't start getting moody and sulking, Friedman," said Stephanie. "You'll spoil everybody's vacation."

"*Some* of us are on vacation," I reminded her. "Some of us are here to find McGovern."

"*All* of us want McGovern to be found," said Stephanie. "The FBI will find him."

"And if they don't?"

"Then you'd *better* find him. But I know you will. Won't he, Baby? Uncle Kinky will find McGovern! Don't worry, darling. Uncle Kinky will be our hero. We'll all be raising our little glasses and shouting, 'Hurray for Dickhead!'"

John McCall was laughing now, a sight I hadn't seen too often. People who are worth over $100 million just don't seem to laugh all that much.

"I'm just picturing those little dogs holding up their little glasses and shouting, 'Hurray for Dickhead!'" said McCall.

Stephanie was laughing now, which was always a beautiful thing to see, and Thisbe and Baby Savannah seemed for all the world to be laughing, too. I considered asking them if they were laughing *at* me or *with* me but, in the interest of mental health, thought better of it. So I laughed along with everybody else, the two little dogs, the gorgeous young woman whom I totally adored and whom I hated to admit was right almost 100 percent of the time, and the man who'd chartered the jet, who currently was keeping a small army of architects gainfully employed building an $18 million estate at Lick Creek outside of Austin, which had been appropriately dubbed the Taj McCall. Why shouldn't I laugh? All I had was an antisocial cat who at this very moment was probably taking lesbian lessons from Winnie. Besides, McGovern had always survived his little adventures in the past. Maybe I would be the one to find him after all.

"Oh, Lordy!" said Stephanie. "This really is too much, Friedman. McGovern's got the luck of the Irish with him. Besides, every stupid investigation you get involved with you end up solving successfully. Usually with my help and guidance, of course."

"Anyway," said McCall, pouring on a little more irritating gentile optimism, "even the person who called you on the phone didn't imply any threat to McGovern. He said, 'Hang loose.' So even the supposed abductor is telling us not to worry."

"Yes," I said, "but you're both overlooking the Man-in-Trouble Hot Line, a system established by McGovern and myself for just such a crisis. McGovern's own words stand in strong opposition to the 'hang loose' salutation. I can still hear him saying, 'MIT—MIT—MIT!!!', sounding desperate, almost beseeching."

"Maybe he ran out of vodka," said Stephanie.

Chapter Twelve

The mood inside the sleek little plane had lightened considerably by the time the lush green countenance of the most beautiful islands in the world came into sight. After all, I reflected, there *were* other explanations for the phenomenon that had occurred. The explanations were tedious, but they were far from tragic. McGovern might've passed out drunk on the beach, for instance, and been recruited as a member of the New Age, homosexual, nudist commune in the rain forests of Kauai. Being a nudist he would, of necessity, have been divested of Hoover's phone number and that was why he hadn't called. Maybe Lono was the New Age name they'd given him. It was also possible that McGovern had tried a large array of those colorful harmless-looking tropical umbrella drinks that sneak up on you and send you rapidly out where the buses don't run. In the process he might've drunken Hoover's phone number. Or he might've not wanted to go back to Hoover's place because he'd met a broad and decided to have a lost weekend in the middle of the week. He could be somewhere near the beach in Honolulu right now locked in a passionate embrace with a large Bulgarian masseuse. As Rambam had once observed: "That's why God made hotels."

"They were originally called the Sandwich Islands," said McCall, as we all gazed down upon a galaxy of green luxuriating in a universe of blue. "Named for the earl of Sandwich."

"Stupid name," said Stephanie.

"Stupid world," I said. "That was the reason Imus once gave me for why he waited so long to get married. He could make his own sandwich, he said."

"Which is more than we can say for you," said Stephanie.

"Why haven't you gotten married yet?" asked McCall. "You could have made some lucky gal a whining, complaining, burping, surly, unpleasant Jewish husband by now."

"Ah," I said, "the ugly head of anti-Semitism raises itself once again."

"That better be the only ugly head that raises itself around here," said Stephanie, looking particularly sensuous. "Why don't you just admit that you're a closet homo?"

"I'll probably become a raging queen some day if you don't marry me."

"Shut up, Friedman! Stop saying perverse things in front of Baby and Thisbe. Uncle Kinky's sorry, darlings. He didn't mean to say bad things. You can marry Mommy, Uncle Kinky," said Stephanie, holding Baby Savannah in front of her and speaking in a squeaky, little voice like a bad ventriloquist. "But first you must promise to *always* obey her. Then you have to have McCall's money, *and* a personality transplant, *and* you have to find McGovern."

"So there's hope," I said.

"It *is* a stupid world," said Stephanie.

The little plane swooped low over the palm trees to make its approach to the small private airport. McCall and I were fastening our seat belts when the ventriloquist began again with Baby's high-pitched expostulations.

"Mommy! Mommy! Look! It's a beach! Can we play on the beach?"

"No, darling, it's too late," said Stephanie in a soothing voice. "We have to go sleepy in our little hotel room. Tomorrow Uncle Kinky will take you and Thisbe out to the beach. After he finds McGovern."

"I don't know about Stephanie's little parlor act with that dog," said McCall. "It could get pretty old pretty fast."

"So could Uncle Kinky," squeaked Baby Savannah.

After that there wasn't much time for conversation by man, woman, or dog. Having narrowly survived a small plane crash in

Alaska, McCall now instinctively developed a rather severe case of the heebie-jeebies upon all takeoffs and landings. This manifested itself by his practically assuming the fetal position, staring frantically through the little cockpit to locate the runway, and screaming, "What's that?!!" at every small noise emanating from the aircraft. This behavior did little to create an atmosphere of comfort amongst his fellow passengers.

It was almost dark by the time we landed at the private airport. We flew through security at a speed faster than even the plane could fly, McCall liberally greasing the wheels with the wad of cash in his pocket he always carried, referring to it casually as "whip-out."

When I saw Hoover standing silently on the tarmac, listlessly holding three brightly colored leis in his hand, I knew something was wrong. He perfunctorily pronounced alohas to Stephanie, McCall, and myself, rather stiffly placing the leis around our necks, and then he pulled me over to one side.

"The cops say they've found the body," he said.

PART THREE

On the Beach

Chapter Thirteen

You can put a couple palm trees in front of it, but a morgue is still a morgue. Like a dog or cat approaching a veterinary clinic, you can almost feel it before you get there. Such was the case as Hoover and I left his little Mazda in the parking lot and walked up to the place. McCall, a subdued Stephanie, and her two *enfants* had taken the limo to the hotel. Identifying the body of a dear friend rarely requires a committee.

"Sorry about this, Kinkyhead," said Hoover, as he held the door to the building. "I know you were close."

"You did your best," I said distractedly. "Maybe if I'd only gotten here sooner—"

"It wouldn't have mattered. From what the cops have told me, McGovern apparently drowned shortly after he disappeared that night."

"Then who said, 'MIT!—MIT!—MIT!' on my telephone three days later?"

"Maybe it was a wrong number."

The place seemed to be humming along with a good bit of activity for a morgue. This wasn't terribly surprising since most morgues are open twenty-four hours and, of course, they don't really have a graveyard shift. The receptionist asked us if we'd please take a seat. She said they'd be right with us. I told her there wasn't any hurry.

"Cops've been wrong before," I said to the fluorescent fixtures in the ceiling. I was having trouble looking at Hoover. He seemed really sad.

"Yeah," he said halfheartedly. "But I don't think they made a mistake this time. They know McGovern's height, weight, age, hair coloring. Everything matches. The time of death and the location of the body all fit the bill, too. Also, there were no other missing persons reported in the area for the time period. If they made a mistake, it's a doozie."

"Everybody makes mistakes," I said, in the vague stupor of tragedy. "I made one about McGovern."

"What was that?"

"Getting too attached."

"That's a mistake with anybody," said Hoover.

"Gentlemen, if you'll come this way," said a prim young man in a lab coat who appeared to walk with at lisp. "We need to talk."

Hoover and I followed the rather officious, sallow-looking fellow into a small office where the temperature had noticeably plummeted a number of degrees. We waited while he fussed with his hair a bit and then rearranged some flowers on his desk. Then, with limpid blue eyes that twinkled a little too much for a morgue attendant, he looked first at me, then at Hoover.

"Which of you," he said, "was his lover?"

"Come again?" I said.

"Is it cold in here or is it me?" said Hoover.

The guy's eyes were sparkling with curiosity now and a slightly prurient sidecar of some other far more incendiary element. Hoover and I glanced briefly at each other. It certainly hadn't been the question we'd expected.

"Before we go any further," he said, "we're going to need an answer to my question."

Hoover and I looked at each other again. This time, whether from general perversity, or whether he genuinely found the situation to be funny, Hoover was smiling like a corpse.

"Why do you ask?" I said finally.

"Because he had sex before he drowned."

"Definitely not McGovern," muttered Hoover.

"This is crazy," I said. "Where's Dr. Quincy?"

"Forensic science," said the lab tech, "is far more sophisticated than it was in, um, Dr. Quincy's time. Traces of sperm were found not only in the stomach but also in the rectum."

"Were there any other distinguishing characteristics," asked Hoover, "other than an asshole big enough to drive a Volkswagen through?"

The light was bright and the guy was pale so it was hard to tell whether he blanched or winced or smiled. Whatever he did, he recovered quickly.

"There is one, um, other distinguishing characteristic," said the guy. "Did your friend have a tattoo of a heart on his right bicep inscribed inside with the word 'Fred'?"

"No!" I shouted unconsciously, like a quiz show contestant. "Mc-Govern lives!"

"Not so fast," said Hoover. "We've come this far. Don't you want to see the stiff?"

"That won't be terribly helpful," said the lab attendant. "He doesn't have a face."

Moments later, out in the parking lot, Hoover and I were laughing loud enough to wake the dead. Tragedy, as so often happens, had turned to comedy in the second act.

"That reminds me of a joke," said Hoover.

"That *was* a joke," I said.

"Well, here's another one. A guy says to his wife, 'Come on. Let's go to bed and have sex.' The wife says 'Okay. But let's not do that finger-in-the-asshole bit tonight.' And the guy says 'Look. It's *my* finger and it's *my* asshole.'"

The rekindling and rebirth of the human spirit can occur in the most unlikely places, such as motels, men's rooms, morgues, in fact almost anywhere other than the Jewish Singles of Dallas Purim Party. Now, as Hoover drove us out toward Diamond Head and the New Otani Kaimana Beach Hotel, the stars indeed sparkled like diamonds and the lights of the city shined like the stars. McGovern was not lying in an oversized ice tray at the morgue. There was hope of finding him alive. There was hope of someday winning the frail, demure hand of Stephanie DuPont. There was hope of getting to the hotel before the bar closed.

"Maybe we'll get back in time to get a big hairy steak at that open-air restaurant under the hau tree where Robert Louis Stevenson once became quite clinically depressed trying to decide whether he was Dr. Jekyll or Mr. Hyde."

"I'm not very hungry," said Hoover. "Visiting a morgue always seems to take away your appetite."

"Not to mention," I said, "your desire to drive a Volkswagen."

Chapter Fourteen

There are two areas of human endeavor that rarely meet with any degree of easy success in Hawaii. One of these is cross-country skiing. The other is the always laborious process of conducting a missing persons investigation. Like the long-gone clouds in the Texas sky of a 1952 photograph of someone you loved, Hawaii has a floating population. An entire midsized city on the mainland could fly into Hawaii and out in the space of a week and never be missed like I miss my mother. Someday, no doubt, we'll all miss our mothers, along with our friends and lovers and anybody else worth a damn in our lives. Either that or everybody else will one day be missing us but they'll probably get over it as all of us must. It's just one of the things that make missing persons work so difficult. As Moses once asked of God upon Mount Sinai: "Why do pets have to conk?" God, according to the Old Testament, did not provide Moses with an answer to his question. He just told him to take two tablets and go to bed.

On the beach bright and early the following morning, I seemed to be having trouble adjusting my eyes. Part of it was the hangover from drinking about nineteen piña coladas the night before at our impromptu little "McGovern Lives!" party. Another part was the blinding beauty of Stephanie DuPont in her bright red strapless tank suit. Every sentient being on the beach was staring at her, including, of course, myself. Thisbe, rather heavy for a Yorkie, was doing her best to waddle through the sand. Baby, however, was scuttling right along like a sand crab in need of Ritalin.

"Tell me," I said to Stephanie, "that you brought along another, somewhat more subdued bathing suit."

"I brought along twenty-five other bathing suits," said Stephanie, helping up Thisbe, who'd sunk halfway into the sand.

"Mother of God!" I ejaculated. "You didn't really bring twenty-six bathing suits."

"Of *course* I did, Dickhead. A girl needs to have choices. Fortunately, one of them isn't you."

"Well, at least we've got everybody's attention. Now maybe we can find somebody who was here five nights ago when McGovern disappeared. You can forget the pale-looking people—"

"Like yourself."

"Anyone who's been here long enough to have been an eyewitness has got to have a tan by now or at least a bad sunburn."

"How about those fagolas over there? They look pretty tan. Maybe you could interview them. How many Speedos did you bring?"

"I just thought of something. None of these tourists would've been on the beach at night anyway."

"That's good, because nobody's taking you seriously in that cornball cowboy hat."

"Maybe they're so struck dumb by your beauty that they can't speak."

Stephanie scooped up Baby Savannah and held her under her chin. It was fairly clear that their little nightclub act was about to begin.

"My mommy's the most beautiful chick on the beach," squeaked Baby Savannah.

"This *could* become very tiresome."

"Shut *up*, Dickhead."

"Mommy wants to know what McGovern was *really* doing in Hawaii," said Baby. "She doesn't think he'd come here just to collect recipes. She thinks he'd be too broke-dick."

"Now that you mention it—"

"I didn't mention it. Baby mentioned it."

"Yes, of course. But Hoover did say something about a free ticket. He wasn't too sure. McGovern had been rather vague about it."

"There you are, Nancy Drew. That could be the key to the whole mystery of McGovern's disappearance."

"The free ticket could well be important," I said. "I'm just hoping nobody tries to punch it."

"We know McGovern's body wasn't the one at the morgue," said Stephanie as she rubbed suntan lotion casually over some achingly beautiful real estate. "But we still don't know dick about where he really is or why. I think we need to let the chicks frolic on the beach a bit, work on our tans, and talk this over from the beginning. We need to come up with a coherent *plan* for finding McGovern. I know the ticket is suspish. We could start there. But you can't wander around in that stooge straw cowboy hat smoking that foul cigar, and asking every tourist you meet if they've seen McGovern. That's varsity pathet!"

"I have a plan, actually. I'll come down here again tonight around midnight, which is about when McGovern was staring down the statue of Duke Kahanamoku, and the last time anyone laid eyes upon him. I'll look for locals, or characters, or lovers on the beach—"

"Oh, *they'll* be happy to see you."

"I also intend for us to visit the state mental hospital this afternoon. Rambam suggested that when the authorities check the hospitals they often don't bother with the mental hospitals. Wig city is exactly where an amnesia victim might turn up."

"Baby Savannah! Get away from the nice lady's book!"

"Maybe she really *likes* Danielle Steel."

"Look, this afternoon we'll check out the mental hospital, and tonight at midnight we'll check out the beach. In the meantime, let's work on our tans and come up with some plans."

"You ever think of becoming a rapper?"

"Baby Savannah! Give the man his headphones back!"

"Maybe she really *likes* Neil Diamond."

"Look, Friedman. Before we go any further with this investigation there's one very important thing you'd better do."

"What is it?"

"Bring me a beach chair."

Chapter Fifteen

The best tool to carry with you into a missing persons investigation is a healthy negative attitude. There had to be a reason why McGovern hadn't gotten in touch with any of us. Hoover hadn't heard from him, I'd had no messages in New York, and Beverly, his live-out girlfriend, hadn't heard a word either and was already fearing the worst. There were, I figured, only three possible explanations for this rather unpleasant set of circumstances. Either McGovern was an amnesia victim, or there'd been foul play and he was being held against his wishes, or he was shark-bait. I didn't like to think about the last possibility, and the notion that several thousand tiny Lilliputians were keeping him captive was fairly ludicrous, so I had to operate on the not-likely assumption that he'd imbibed about ninety-seven tropical drinks, fallen down and hit his head, and was now blithering around someplace, walking on his knuckles, looking for his zip code. The only problem with this theory was that, according to Hoover, he'd been stone sober the last time he'd seen him. And then there was that strange phone call.

It was quite a three-cigar problem and if it were to be resolved successfully I'd have to maintain a clear and focused overview of the whole situation. Hoover could handle the liaison with the cops and McCall could deal with the initials. My feeling was that if the powers that be were going to solve this case they would've done it already. It was going to require, I figured, not only an intimate knowledge of Mc-Govern's brain, but also a savvy grasp upon human nature, a field of study of which I'd become grudgingly more aware the older I got. And I was already old enough to be on guard against nose hairs with the judicious employment of battery-operated nose-hair clippers. I was old enough to miss a cat. I was old enough to miss a friend.

After bringing Stephanie her beach chair, I withdrew to the lanai of my room, which had become, as far as I was concerned, the spiritual headquarters of the investigation. I had a suite with a partial ocean view, from which you could see the ocean and the green hillsides of the island, sit in the sun on the lanai, drink Kona coffee, smoke a Cuban cigar, and call anyone you liked on the blower. The view I liked best was just in my sight, a splash of fire engine red in a pale green beach chair on the shimmering white sand near the emerald-blue ocean. This was the perfect place to put pieces of a puzzle together. Unfortunately, there were damn few pieces to work with. If some kind of cohesive picture did not emerge very soon there would be more than mere trouble in paradise. If the forces of nature or foul play were involved, and I was leaning heavily toward the latter, Mc-Govern might well by now have gone to Jesus. If he was alive, it was incumbent upon me to use my head for something other than a hatrack. If rational deductive reasoning and good ol' American cowboy logic failed me now, I might lose my favorite Irish poet forever.

I called Beverly in New York and verified, after some rather tedious hand-holding, that McGovern had indeed hinted at having a free ticket to Hawaii. He had not invited her along and she hadn't wanted to pry, just assuming that he needed to be on his own for a while. Now she blamed herself for letting him go. I told her that Mc-Govern had been alone in some mighty out-of-the-way places before, including a long solo stand in Roratonga. I told her I was sure he'd be getting in touch with us all soon, though by this time, I was seriously doubting that would happen.

I called Hoover next and and asked him to check through McGovern's possessions for his airline ticket and get back to me. Hoover had heard nothing from the cops. I asked him if he wanted to come along with us to the mental hospital that afternoon. He said no, he already worked in a mental hospital. It was called a major metropolitan news-paper. Hoover did agree to join us that night on the beach to show us where the cops had found the big man's recipe book.

"There's another reporter here," said Hoover, "who wants to talk to you about this investigation."

"Put him on."

"First of all, it's not a he. Her name is Carline Ravel and she's a real looker."

"Put her on."

"Second of all, she's not here right now. She's covering a story on the Big Island. Is it okay if I have her call you at the hotel?"

"Why not? We seem to be going absolutely nowhere at the moment. What's her angle?"

"It's pretty strange. Even a little spooky maybe. I doubt if it's going to be any help anyway. But I promised her I'd let her tell you."

"Fine," I said. "Nobody's told me anything since I got here except Stephanie. She told me to bring her a beach chair."

"And you did, of course. I'll bet every guy on the beach was jealous as hell."

"You get used to it."

I fired up a fresh cigar, poured a new head on my cup of Kona coffee, and looked out at the city and the sea. Kona coffee, when imported to the mainland, never tastes nearly as good as it does on the islands. Even the coffee served at Denny's by the Sea just down the way from our hotel beat any gourmet grind in the world. McGovern missing almost a week and I'm sitting on a luxurious lanai overlooking Stephanie DuPont's red tank suit eating sushi with chopsticks and that hot green stuff that I can never remember is called wasabi, so I usually call it Yosemite Sam and they know what I mean. Just like ordering a big hairy steak and asking for Gestapo sauce because I can't remember Tabasco and they bring it anyway. They don't care if you choke to death or hang yourself masturbating; as long as you've got the bucks they bring it anyway, whatever it is and whoever they are.

It was tragic really that paradise should go on with McGovern missing almost a week. Maybe we'd all been in denial and that was why we were so slow to grasp the gravity of the situation. Now, like the tide and the tourists, the candle of hope was going out and the answers had flown away. There were no leads. There were no clues except the possible free airline ticket. There were no ransom demands.

On the positive side of the ledger was McGovern's own voice saying, "MIT!—MIT!—MIT!!," over the blower almost three nights ago. At that time McGovern was alive but he knew he was a man in trouble. Had someone coerced my phone number from him to tell me to hang loose, that everything was okay, that McGovern wouldn't be harmed? Or was McGovern trying to tell me something else entirely? McGovern's very life, I now realized, could hang in the balance of how I interpreted the message on the blower. And with every wave that washed the sand I was running out of time to interpret.

I was contemplating impaling myself upon Stephanie's beach chair twelve stories below when the figure of John McCall suddenly appeared behind my left shoulder and almost caused me to leap sideways off the lanai.

"Never sneak up on a veteran," I said, retrieving my cigar from the sandy floor.

"You weren't answering the door so I got the maid to let me in," he said. "What do you think of these?"

He slammed a sheaf of posters into my hand, each bearing McGovern's smiling face along with the word "Missing" at the top, a 1-800 phone number, and the mention of a large reward at the bottom. I knew it was necessary and routine in missing persons investigations to paper a city with missing posters the same way you might if you lost your cat. It just seemed like such a pathetic last-resort tactic that it brought home the futility of our efforts thus far and served to depress me enormously. And all the while those Irish eyes kept smiling.

"Jesus," I said. "It's enough to snap me out of any denial I had left. When do we put them up?"

"They're already going up all over town," said McCall. "I just spread a little whip-out around with the hotel employees this morning. It's being taken care of. At least it may put a little pressure on whoever's holding McGovern and maybe they'll contact us."

"So you think he's been kidnapped?"

"Judging from the phone call to you before we left, the lack of any further communication from McGovern, and the lack of a body, I'd say, hell yes, he's been kidnapped."

"Then why hasn't there been a ransom demand?"

"Maybe there will be one."

"As they say in snorkeling, 'Don't hold your breath.'"

Chapter Sixteen

Even with a whole plantation of palm trees in front of it, a mental hospital is still a mental hospital. Wherever it is in the world, the heavy, desperate air of wig city floats out to suffocate with sadness the casual visitor to the freak show. You come to see but you never come to know. This is as true today in Hawaii as it was in Zelda Fitzgerald's "sanitarium," which mysteriously burned to the ground one night with Jesus, Napoléon, and Zelda still inside. Rather cosmically, in an irony that F. Scott himself might've appreciated, the locus for this conflagration was Asheville, North Carolina. Visitors to the site nowadays report that they can still feel the anguish of the ashes in this Auschwitz of the mind.

"This place gives me the creeps," said Stephanie, as we walked up the drive. "I'm glad I decided to leave Thisbe and Baby Savannah at the hotel."

"So am I," muttered McCall.

"Too bad you and Baby couldn't perform your ventriloquist act in there for some of the shrinks," I said, as several obviously deranged people strolled by. "They'd lock us all up and throw away the key."

"It might be a good educational experience for both of you," said Stephanie, nodding toward a sign near the door. "At least you two old senile fucks would know that today is Thursday and that the next meal is supper."

"Have I ordered yet?" said McCall.

"I'm serious," whispered Stephanie. "This place is damned *spooky*."

"Have I *eaten* yet?" said McCall.

There is something about the internal structure of every wig city that appears to make that institution eerily similar to the one in the movie *One Flew Over the Cuckoo's Nest.* Maybe wig city personnel have seen the film and in one way or another overidentified with the various characters. Be that as it may, the Nurse Ratched role was well handled by a large officious woman who seemed to have difficulty in grasping the precise nature of our little visit. Stephanie and John took up chairs in the visitors' area as I ankled it over to the desk at the nurse's station.

"I called earlier to arrange a brief tour of the hospital—"

"No one informed me. Are you visiting a patient?"

"I'm looking for a friend," I said.

"I see," said Nurse Ratched, removing her rather austere skepticals to reveal a pair of rather austere blue eyes. "What makes you think your friend is a patient here?"

"Because he disappeared almost a week ago and he doesn't seem to be anywhere else."

"That cigar isn't lit, is it?" she said sharply.

"No, it isn't. He could be a victim of amnesia."

"*Who* could be a victim of amnesia?"

"My friend."

"I see," said the woman, giving no indication that she did. She shuffled papers randomly for a few moments.

"What's *taking* so long?" said Stephanie, her shrill voice reaching me like an arrow in the back. I turned around to placate my mutinous troops.

"Hold the weddin'!" I said.

"That's *one* thing you won't have to worry about," she said.

I turned back around and smiled at the big nurse with whatever charm I still had in stock. She did not smile back.

"What's your friend's name?" asked the woman as she studied my straw cowboy hat. She did not seem to be enjoying her field of study.

"Michael R. McGovern," I said. "But, of course, he wouldn't know that." Maybe I would get rid of the cowboy hat, I thought.

"How do *you* know that *he* wouldn't know?" said the woman, like a suspicious wife catching her husband in a lie.

"If he has amnesia," I said with some frustration, "he wouldn't know his name."

"Are you a doctor?" asked the woman in a mild yet infuriating manner.

"What's *taking* so long?" shouted Stephanie.

The bureaucratic blue eyes of the nurse locked on for a long moment with the imperious blue eyes of my blond companion. McCall and I stood by like innocent passersby watching in horror. Men can little fathom what goes on in the silken machinery behind blue eyes and besides, neither McCall nor myself wanted to get involved. Nobody in his right mind likes a catfight in a mental hospital.

"I'm not a doctor," I said at last. "I'm a man attempting to visit a mental hospital. I called earlier and I thought everything was set up but apparently the lines were down—"

There was no point in continuing. There was no longer anyone behind the desk. The woman had obviously retired into her little rabbit warren leaving me there talking to myself like a mental patient with an imaginary friend. It was a rather embarrassing situation, but considering where it was taking place it could hardly be thought of as an odd event.

John and Stephanie were on their feet and I was lighting my cigar in the lobby in preparation to leave the building when a highly agitato individual in a phlegm-colored jumpsuit came jumping through his asshole toward us. At first I figured his excitement was caused by the standard pathetically predictable reaction in most institutions, mental or otherwise, to the wholly unacceptable circumstance of man lighting cigar in lobby. Then I changed my mind and lamped him for a mental patient coming to kill me. I was, as fate would have it, wrong on both counts.

"Hi! I'm Kimo!" he said, leering violently at Stephanie. "Ready, folks? The grand tour of the zoo is leaving now!"

True to his words, the orderly lurched forward immediately into the bowels of the building. We followed his large, swaying buttocks down a long, curving, vaguely nightmarish corridor through which indeed reverberated sounds that seemed far from human.

"I'm *really* glad I left the chicks at the hotel," said Stephanie.

"I wish you'd left me there, too," said John.

"You two are behaving like squeamish, sheltered little babies," I said. "There's virtually no difference between the insanity within these walls and the quiet desperation outside them. It's all a mere matter of degrees of human behavior, virtually all of which is patently ludicrous in the eyes of God, history, or a large, intelligent, mildly observant dog. Many of these people will be us in a few years and many of us will be them."

Suddenly, a pale, naked figure, sporting only a macadamia nut necklace and a monstro-erection, darted across the hallway and vanished again, screaming, "Catch me if you can!" in a very ill falsetto. Fast on his heels, an orderly in a phlegm-colored jumpsuit shouted, "Albert! Stop or I'll take away your Beanie Babies!"

"That'll be Kinky in two years," said Stephanie.

"Not me," I said. "I hate Beanie Babies. If I see one I try to hang it upside-down and mutilate its genitalia."

"That'll be Kinky in two *weeks*," said Stephanie.

"It could happen," said McCall in a sudden serious tone, "if he doesn't find McGovern."

Informing Kimo, our modern-day Virgil, that we were only interested in seeing patients who'd been admitted within the past week, served to somewhat abbreviate the tour. After checking out several McGovernless dayrooms, Kimo proceeded to show us a large ward filled entirely with Japanese. It wasn't clear if any of their number believed themselves to be Hirohito instead of Napoléon, but one patient in particular came up to us and bowed repeatedly in a highly excitable manner. When he spoke, his accent and intonation were remarkably similar to that of a prison guard in an old Hollywood World War II movie.

"Herp me! Herp me get out of here!" he shouted in a staccato, machine-gunlike voice. "Honolable vis-i-tah! I-am-*not*-Jap-a-nese!"

There is a pervasive sadness to any wig city, and part of this I attribute to the presence of Jesus. Many of its inhabitants believe themselves to be Jesus, suspect they may be Jesus, or are at least highly conversant with Jesus on a first-name basis. This is dangerous spiritual territory for anyone who isn't a politician, a football coach, or a televangelist. It is also my long-held belief, however, that Jesus may indeed be communicating with these people, secure in the knowledge that the rest of us idiots will never believe them.

If Jesus was undeniably dwelling at wig city, it was becoming increasingly clear to me that McGovern wasn't. In fact, the whole amnesia scenario was quickly fading from my mind as a viable possibility. But what was left? It was like seeing an object far ahead of you and not yet knowing if it's only a large piece of cardboard flapping in the wind or a large brown dog contorting in hypnotizingly horrible death throes on the shoulder of the highway or merely the end of the world.

Just as Kimo was starting to lead us out into the sunshine, away from the stale perfume of antiseptic anonymity, desperation, and despair, we passed an admissions office where a rather riveting scene was taking place. As much as I wanted the trade winds to wash the grime of humanity from my fevered brow, I felt the need to just one more time stare into the abyss. So we loitered outside the doorway for a moment and overheard a final snatch of conversation between a man who could clearly be categorized as incoming wounded and another man who was apparently a staff shrink.

"I'm going to fucking kill myself!" shouted the new admission. "I'm going to fucking kill myself!"

"You'll do nothing of the sort," said the shrink calmly. "I want you to take your meds and relax, and this afternoon we have a wonderful treat. The circus is in town and Bozo the Clown is coming by to give us a special matinee show. You just watch Bozo the Clown for a little while and, believe me, your heart will feel considerably lighter."

"Doctor," said the man. "I *am* Bozo the Clown."

Chapter Seventeen

"**What do you mean** you can't find his plane ticket?" I said. It was earlier that afternoon and I was at missing persons' command central on my lanai with a piña colada in one hand, a cigar in the other, and my eyes burning bright as Robert Louis Stevenson's as I watched the waves rolling further back than the pictures of my grandparents that I kept in my head.

"I can't find his *plane* ticket," Hoover repeated, this time quite a bit louder.

"Maybe he had an electronic ticket," I said.

"No, I saw the damn ticket myself at baggage claim at the airport when he got here. And I know he didn't have it on him the night he disappeared. All his stuff's still at my place—his suitcase, toilet kit, passport, address book. But the plane ticket's not there."

"Go back and look through his stuff again. Ask yourself, if I were a plane ticket where would I be?"

"I've already searched through his shit seven times," said Hoover. "If it's not bad enough that McGovern's missing in action, now his fucking *plane* ticket's disappeared as well."

"And what does this suggest to you, my dear Watson?"

"It suggests that if we don't find McGovern and his ticket soon I'll probably lose my mind and my job. I don't care about my mind so much, but newspaper work's hard to find these days."

"So's McGovern," I said. "And if I don't find him we'll all be out of a job."

"Which would be pretty difficult for you since you've never had a job in your life."

"There's where you're very wrong, Watson. I do have a job. It's simply not demarcated by hours of the day or night nor compensated by financial reward. My only employers, Watson, are my brains and the limitless vistas of my imagination."

"I wasn't talking about a hand job," said Hoover.

After about four hours of dark chuckling, I was able to suck, fuck, and cajole Hoover into a midnight rendezvous at the statue of Duke Kahanamoku. It was the last place and the last time McGovern had been seen alive. It was where I intended to begin the proactive portion of the investigation. I doubted seriously if the cops, the tourists, and the tide had left any clues remaining on the beach, but possibly some of its habitual denizens might still be loitering around.

There wasn't much left of the afternoon and there was even less information coming in from the cops, through Hoover, or the FBI, via McCall. The missing plane ticket gave me a little pause but, like dogs and cats, plane tickets do occasionally go missing, not unlike, in certain exceptional circumstances, their owners.

It was nearing sunset when I put in a call to Rambam's shoe phone, got no response, and left a message on his badly tapped line in New York. You could hear a metallic clicking noise every time you talked to Rambam, which he contended was the sound of the FBI. Very possibly he was correct. With the FBI monitoring Rambam's line so closely, it was understandable, I reflected, that they hadn't had time to come up with much on McGovern. J. Edgar Hoover had already woken up in hell next to Oscar Wilde, which undoubtedly caused Oscar some mild displeasure, but Hoover's legacy lived on. Though dangerous individuals like Martin Luther King, John Lennon, and Leonard Bernstein had gone to Jesus and could no longer be effectively spied upon, there were other threats to the government that would take their places as targets of the feds. The FBI would always be better at these surreptitious, vicarious activities than they ever would at a task as simple as finding my favorite Irish poet. There was something about the FBI that didn't like a poet.

As the flaming orb of the sun began to cool its red-hot tail in the calm Pacific, Stephanie and I and the two *enfants* watched from my oceanfront suite. Stephanie, I noticed, was quickly developing a gorgeous apricot tan. It seemed to go particularly nicely with the cute little peach-colored tank suit she was wearing. There were, I reflected, many things I wouldn't have minded seeing on Stephanie. One of them, of course, was myself.

"Everyone on the beach has been giving Thisbe food," she said. "By the time she leaves here she's going to look like a little sumo wrestler."

"She already looks like a little sumo wrestler," I said. "See the way she's eyeballing those purple-colored poi rolls on the coffee table?"

"Baby's been out on the beach searching for McGovern. It's really kind of sad that we can't do *something*."

"We're going to do something. I've been trying to find people's numbers in my old black telephone book, but the damn thing's about three inches thick and half the people in it are dead."

"That's natural for an old man like yourself. In fact, it's not entirely bad. It just means you've outlived half the people you've known in your life."

"Yeah," I said. "But it's the wrong half."

As we watched the most beautiful sunset in the world I made a little silent prayer that Mike McGovern would not join the half of my phone book inhabitants who'd had their numbers call-forwarded to the sky. I knew from previous work with Rambam that missing persons investigations moved at sometimes leisurely, sometimes frantic, sometimes frustrating paces, almost as if they had minds of their own. No matter how many buttons you pushed or bases you covered the most important things were to keep an alert, open mind, keep your professional poise, and keep yourself in the saddle until you rode the bastard into the ground. There was a natural rhythm to these cases that could take a few hours or could take a few years, and to attempt to interrupt or manipulate that rhythm was always a fool's game. You just had to go with the flow, and in Hawaii it was all around you.

"Watch the sunset," I said. "You might see the green flash."

"The only green flash I've seen lately is McCall showing off his whip-out."

"What I'm referring to is a natural phenomenon, sort of Hawaii's version of the aurora borealis. What causes the green flash, only scientists know. What it signifies, only kahunas know. Why people like us sit here and watch for it, only God knows. Because if you're looking for it, it almost never happens."

"I hope we find McGovern," said Stephanie.

"Me, too, darling."

"It just seems so difficult here. We don't know the people, the police, the land, the customs. In New York, with all your stupid friends helping out, you'd probably have found him by now. Here, it could take forever. Maybe we shouldn't have come."

"Sexually?"

"That's *never* been funny, Friedman. Especially at a time like this. Admit it. Maybe you've bitten off more than you can chew."

"We had to come out here," I said. "We all love McGovern. Now that we're here—"

"—and nothing's happening—"

"Don't be too sure that nothing's happening. The islands are deceptively peaceful, but that could change in a heartbeat. It might take a bit longer for our efforts to bear fruit because the environment is so foreign to us. I've never conducted a criminal investigation in paradise before. It all feels very strange and unfamiliar."

"Well, you know what my father always says."

"I haven't the faintest idea."

"Never order a margarita in a Chinese restaurant," said Stephanie.

Not wishing to appear critical of her father, I merely nodded appreciatively and continued to watch as the sun disappeared below the watery horizon. There was no reason to challenge her father's wisdom. There was no time to waste in the investigation. There was no green flash.

Chapter Eighteen

"Mahalo," said the parking valet, as Hoover dropped off his car at the hotel that night.

Though circumstances were beginning to look decidedly dire, it was a good feeling to finally be about to inspect the ostensible scene of the crime. It was true that time, tides, and tourists had come and gone, but I still retained hopes of finding an eyewitness to McGovern's disappearance. According to Hoover, McGovern had been wearing a bright blue, rather distinctive aloha shirt with tall green-and-yellow palms running its entire length, which, in McGovern's case, was considerable.

"Mother of God," I said, as Stephanie, Hoover, and I walked down Kalakaua Avenue toward Waikiki. "That's the shirt I once gave him from one of my earlier trips here."

"With your record as an Indian giver," said Stephanie, "that's probably a good omen. Maybe the shirt will come back to you with McGovern in it."

"I'm not so sure," I said grimly. "I bought that shirt at the Royal Hawaiian Hotel. The guy who sold it to me assured me that it was a precise replica of the shirt Montgomery Clift died in in *From Here to Eternity*."

"That's probably not a good omen," said Hoover. "By the way, where's your millionaire buddy McCall? Why isn't he out here helping us scour the beach?"

"First of all," I said, "he's not a millionaire. He's a centimillionaire. He has over $100 million—"

"And he let a broke-dick like you pick up the check last night."

"That's why he's a centimillionaire," I said. "But to answer your question, Hoover, he's currently in his suite assiduously monitoring the CIA, who are assiduously monitoring the DEA, who are probably busy arresting somebody's marijuana plant in Maui."

No matter how dark life looks, there is something about walking from Diamond Head down to Waikiki along colorful Kalakaua Avenue that invariably lifts your spirits. Possibly it's the beach and the ocean, which run the length of Kalakaua like a faithful friend. Possibly it's the transitory happiness of the transitory people. Possibly it's the fact that King Kalakaua himself lifted a lot of spirits in his lifetime. According to Robert Louis Stevenson, the Merry Monarch once drank five bottles of champagne before breakfast. Afterward, again according to RLS, there was no change in the king's appearance or demeanor except that he became "perceptibly more dignified." Some of Kalakaua's spirit, indeed, now seemed to have infected Will Hoover.

"There once was a man named Gandhi," he recited. "Who woke up one day with a dandy."

"That's not even *vaguely* amusing," said Stephanie.

"He said to his aide, fetch me a maid, or a goat, or anything handy."

"That was horrendous," said Stephanie. "I'm glad I left the chicks at the hotel."

"So am I," said Hoover.

"I wish we'd left *your* ass at the hotel," said Stephanie.

"Please," I said. "We must have no rancor in the ranks at this crucial phase of the investigation."

"Investigation, my sweet rebel ass," said Stephanie with no small amount of scorn. "When is it supposed to start?"

"She's right, Kinkyhead," said Hoover. "We haven't found one clue or one trace of McGovern yet."

"Wrong you are, my dear Watson," I said. "But there's no time to go into that now. If I'm not very much mistaken that's the statue of Duke Kahanamoku standing just in front of us."

"It's pretty hard to miss, Dickhead," said Stephanie. "It's the only statue on the whole length of the beach and it's about five times bigger than God."

"So it is," I said rather distractedly. "And now, Hoover, if you will stand precisely in the same place where you last saw McGovern."

"I can't," said Hoover.

"Why not, Watson?"

"Because that long white limo full of Japanese tourists will run over my body."

"Good," said Stephanie. "We wouldn't have to hear any more of your stupid limericks."

I waited until the limo passed. Then I walked onto the empty street in front of the statue. The first thing that caught my eye was the cop shop located just to the right of the statue.

"Christ on a Boogie Board," I said. "You never told me there was a cop shop this close to the statue."

"You never asked me," said Hoover. "What does it mean, O great Kinkyhead?"

"Yeah, what does it mean, Dickhead?" said Stephanie. "You'd have to be pretty ballsy to kidnap somebody this close to a police station."

"It certainly suggests a different way of looking at things," I said. "Now, Hoover. Cast your mind back to that fateful night. First, did you actually see McGovern walking to the beach? And second, can you take us to the place where you found his notes on the cookbook?"

"No to the first question," said Hoover. "Yes to the second."

"Then what are we waiting for?" I said, as I used the Duke's giant surfboard to shield the ignition of a fresh cigar. "Lead on, Watson!"

Chapter Nineteen

It wasn't Bali Hai. It wasn't Iwo Jima. It wasn't Normandy. It was just a public beach at night after the public had gone away. Now it was just the sands of Hertz Rent-a-Car. The sands of McDonald's. The sands of Sheraton, Hilton, and Hyatt. The sad sands of American loneliness that had once been part of a great primeval rock, now reduced to weathering wandering footprints no eye would ever see, no heart ever follow. It was just an empty beach caught in a darkened hourglass between the twinkling lights of the careless city and the phosphorescent reflections of the eternal sea.

"Kind of spooky," said Hoover. "Looks like a good place for the *menehune* to come out."

"Who're the *menehune?*" asked Stephanie.

"They're little leprechaun-like creatures who the Hawaiians believe come out late at night to cause mischief."

"Like you and Hoover," said Stephanie, rising like a goddess of the sea to her full height of five-eleven and a half and glaring down upon the two of us.

"Maybe another limerick's in order," said Hoover.

"Maybe my strangling your ass is in order," said Stephanie. "We're not going to find anything on this fucking beach anyway. There's not a living soul anywhere around."

"That's not entirely true," said Hoover, motioning into the darkness. "What about that guy?"

We could now clearly see the bent-over figure of an old man shuffling along the water's edge, slowly scanning the sand with a metal detector. As he came closer he looked for all the world like a prophet from the pages of the Bible, or today's version of the same individual, a man from a homeless shelter. He was a "poi" man. His ancestry was a mixed bag, the result of several hundred years of fun and sun on the islands. If we looked deep enough into the past we'd probably determine that all of us, with the possible exception of that frail little Aryan flower Stephanie DuPont, are "poi" people. It's one of the things that had made Hawaii magical and America great.

Before I knew it, with the sure touch of a skilled reporter and interviewer, Hoover was over conversing with the old man. They seemed to be communicating in a pidgin dialect, employing some English, some Hawaiian, and a great many gestures with the hands, the head, even including the old man pointing several times with his lips, a rather unusual custom I hadn't observed since my Peace Corps days in the jungles of Borneo. In Borneo it's considered rude to point with your hand. Most of our mothers taught us the same thing when we were children. What the civilized West forgets, the primitive East remembers.

"He saw McGovern," shouted Hoover excitedly. "He recognizes him from the picture!"

Hoover promptly folded up the missing poster and returned to a rather animated conversation with the old man.

"This is better than we could've expected," I said to Stephanie. "The gods of missing coins and missing persons seem to be with us."

"We'll see," said Stephanie doubtfully.

"He went that way!" shouted Hoover, pointing toward the pink picturesque structure of the Royal Hawaiian Hotel, the oldest hotel on the beach. "He left with a wahine!"

"What's a wahine?" asked Stephanie.

"A woman," I said.

"A babe?"

"Not as beautiful as you, I'm sure."

"Everything's relative," said Stephanie, as she tossed her long blond, rich-girl hair toward the beckoning sea. "I wasn't being vain. I was just wondering if she was attractive enough to seduce McGovern."

"The answer is yes," I said. "To McGovern anything with two legs and a vagina—"

"Friedman! I'm warning you!"

"—is a babe. Anyone under fifty is young. Any woman with a job is independently wealthy. In other words, any wahine could've probably picked him up."

"That doesn't say much for McGovern."

"On the contrary, it says quite a bit. He insists that the woman be kind, compassionate, courteous, intelligent, generous, and reasonably clean."

"Why doesn't he just pick up a Boy Scout?" said Stephanie.

"They're too thrifty," I said.

At last we were making some headway, I felt. The wahine angle explained a number of things. It accounted for how McGovern could've been so easily abducted in the first place. It accounted for how he could've been spirited away from a vicinity only a stone's throw from a cop shop. It also possibly accounted for why nobody'd heard from him initially. But it did not account for the worrisome MIT—MIT—MIT phone call I'd received. Nor did it explain McGovern's total lack of communication since then.

By the time Hoover had finished with the old man, all of us were definitely aware that we at least had a lead. A lead is something that you hope you can follow. It doesn't always take you where you want to go, but it's better than watching a naked man with a large erection running through a mental hospital.

"We're hot on the scent," said Hoover cheerfully. "It puts me in mind of a limerick I know."

"Oh, Lordy!" said Stephanie. "Can't you shut him up, Friedman?"

"I wouldn't dream of it."

"There once was a pervert named Hoover," began Hoover. "Who knew a sex fiend in Vancouver."

"I don't want to *hear* it!" said Stephanie.

"She was a lascivious young slut—"

"He's got Tourette's syndrome," said Stephanie.

"Plus she had a big butt—"

"Can't you *stop* him, Friedman?"

"No."

"And she taught him the Hind-lick maneuver," finished Hoover with a flourish.

"That was horrendous," said Stephanie.

"What do we do now, Sherlock?" said Hoover, smiling obliviously.

"We buy you a muzzle for Christmas," said Stephanie.

"Did the old guy give you a description of the wahine?" I asked Hoover. "Features? Hair coloring? Height? Was she as tall as Stephanie, for instance?"

"*Nobody's* as tall as Stephanie," said Hoover.

"And don't *forget* it," said Stephanie. "You little *mehuna*."

"It's *menehune*," said Hoover. "Now a *mehuna* is a rather arcane device that is placed upon the crotch of a wahine—"

"Friedman! This is too much!" shouted Stephanie. "I'm going back to the hotel to check on *les enfants*."

But before she could make good on her threat, a dark figure came running down the beach toward us. As the figure came closer it gradually materialized into John McCall. He seemed to be highly agitato.

"How did you find us?" I asked.

"I just ran down to the statue and followed the cigar smoke," said John.

"We just got a lead," said Hoover.

"We just got something else, too," said McCall.

"What?" said Stephanie, a note of dread dropping into her voice.

"A ransom note," said McCall.

PART FOUR

On the Money

Chapter Twenty

The only place you can get really bad coffee in Hawaii is at Starbucks. If you stay away from there you pretty much can't go wrong. Room service at any fancy hotel or flophouse, fine restaurants, or Denny's by the Sea, even the Forty-Nine Diner (so named because everybody thought Hawaii would be the forty-ninth state of the union and everybody was wrong)—all serve killer-bee coffee employing varying amounts of Jack and the Beanstalk's magic Kona bean. It's beyond a doubt the drink of choice if you're waiting for kidnappers to reestablish communication with you on a ransom demand.

The ransom note itself was a rather simple and straightforward affair. The kidnappers obviously had seen the "Missing" posters, called the phone number at the hotel desk, then, rather than putting the call through as per our instructions, simply hung up and decided to drop off the ransom note instead. What, if anything, this indicated at this early stage, was anybody's guess.

The ransom note read as follows: "We have your friend. Do as instructed and no one gets hurt. Collect $50,000 in small, used bills. No fifties or hundreds. Wait for further instructions. If you contact the police, your friend is dead. P.S.: Don't call us. We'll call you."

It was getting into the wee hours of the morning by this time and I was pouring coffee, poring over the ransom note, and praying that Rambam would return one of my four phone calls to him before the kidnappers contacted me again. Everything had suddenly shifted into a higher gear, into a mode of mild hysteria, into a situation in which a slight miscue or minor oversight could result in dire consequences indeed.

In my fairly limited experience as an amateur private investigator, I'd never dealt with a circumstance in which I personally had ever received an actual ransom note, a clear-cut, concrete threat to the life of someone close to me. I was as ill-equipped and unsure of how to handle this as Lindbergh no doubt had been in his day. For the moment, I figured, I'd follow the directions of the note meticulously. I'd continue to drink coffee, I'd continue to feed the birds on my lanai the purple-colored poi rolls they seemed to like even though every hotel in Honolulu had signs posted that read: "Please Don't Feed the Birds. *Mahalo.*" For the moment, I'd continue to wait for either Rambam or the kidnappers to call, and I planned to do whatever either of them suggested, whichever came first. I would not contact the police.

I'd already delegated the task of getting the ransom money together to John McCall. If you happen to have a centimillionaire traveling with you, he's usually the best man for the job. To John, coming up with a $50,000 ransom was roughly comparable to anybody else flipping a coin to a minstrel boy. The amount of money had seemed surprisingly low to me, but it's always a good idea not to try to get too deeply into the mind of a kidnapper. The best policy, I felt, was to sit tight, wait for them to call, and keep feeding the birds.

In most places, birds are asleep late at night in their little nests, dreaming of worms, or fanciful flights, or tropical paradises. In Hawaii, birds, and pigeons as well, operate on a much more flexible schedule. If room service is happening twenty-four hours, so are the birds. If they see a large mammal pacing back and forth on his lanai with a dark twig in his hand and smoke periodically puffing out of his mouth, they know something might be up. If the large mammal is breaking up poi rolls and scattering the crumbs across the floor of the lanai, word gets around pretty quickly. On wings of dreams they flock to the large mammal in the night, never knowing the turmoil in his heart.

Feathers were flapping and pigeons were crapping and the next thing I knew it was two-thirty in the morning and the phones were ringing inside my room. I ran to the nearest blower, which happened

to be in the dumper, and collared it tightly and swiftly, my hand like
the talon of a hawk sweeping in on its prey.

"Start talkin'," I said.

"Let's hear the ransom note," said Rambam calmly. Hearing his
voice had a calming effect on me, too. If anybody could tell me how to
deal with this situation it was Rambam.

I lowered the lid on the dump machine and sat down. Then I read
him the note. He didn't say anything for a moment and I had the rather
unsettling notion that he might've nodded off. At last he spoke.

"Well, you know what you have to do," he said.

"Of *course* I don't know what I have to do. I don't have any *idea*
what to do. That's why I left you four urgent messages."

"You've got to go to the cops," said Rambam.

"'If you contact the police,'" I read aloud from the note, "'your
friend is dead.'"

"There's a fair chance, Kinky, that that's already the case. You've
got to be prepared for that possibility."

"But you don't personally think that McGovern's dead?"

"I personally think that when it gets as far as ransom notes all bets
are off. You know I'm allergic to cops, but they're the only ones with
the ability and the manpower to trap and trace. You can't go after kidnappers these days on a foot-pedaled rickshaw."

"Okay, I'll bring in the cops. What's trap and trace?"

"It's just like in the movies. They trace the call to an individual
phone and trap the kidnapper. Trap and trace."

"Then it should be trace and trap."

"It should be roll 'n' rock, too. But tell the cops trap and trace and
they'll think you speak their language and maybe they'll move faster.
Call 'em as soon as you hang up with me. I'm coming out there myself
in a few days."

"That's great," I said, mildly surprised by the flood of relief I felt.
"Where are you now?"

"I'm at the airport in Paris about to fly to Morocco to investigate a
case of grand theft camel."

"I see," I said. "But you'll get here as soon as you can?"

"Sure," said Rambam. "But I'm telling you, once it's in the hands
of the cops, there won't be much for me to do."

"You're being modest," I said. "You can help me pedal the rick-shaw."

I cradled the blower with Rambam and I ankled it out of the rain room. Then I poured another cup of coffee. Then I fired up a fresh cigar. Then I called the cops.

Chapter Twenty-one

The unaimed arrow never misses, they say in Hawaii. It's a little kahuna Zen secret that the haoles on the mainland haven't picked up on yet and, from the looks of things, probably never will. It means if you don't focus too intently upon something you want, you might just have a rat's ass chance in hell of getting it. It also means that things move slowly in Hawaii, but when they really start to move you need to take your Jimmy Buffett flip-flops and your little umbrella drink and get the hell out of the way. You need to leap sideways before your karma runs its surfboard over your dogma.

I was taking a little power nap, waiting for the cops to arrive, when the phones rang. A phone by the bed and a phone in the dumper is never quite the same thing as having two red blowers on opposite sides of your desk, but it's one of the situations you put up with on the road. Like giving up your goose-feather bed to sleep on the cold, cold ground beside your gypsy rover. Like giving up watching a dark-colored pigeon shitting on a rusty fire escape for watching a white-colored pigeon in a palm tree shitting on your head. They say that any bird shitting on your head is invariably an omen of good luck. I suppose that's what I was half-hoping for and half-dreaming about when the phones rang. I picked up the blower by the bed.

"Start talkin'," I said.

"Aloha," said a sultry-sounding woman's voice. "Am I calling too late?"

"Who wants to know?" I said.

"This is Carline Ravel, Hoover's friend from the *Honolulu Advertiser*. I'm still over here on the Big Island but he said I could call you at any time. He said you're a dreamer who never sleeps."

"He stole that from Captain Midnight," I said. I was suddenly aware that I wanted the phone lines free in case the kidnappers should call.

"I think I've stumbled on something that may help you find your friend," she said.

I was wide awake now. This was the broad Hoover had mentioned might possibly have some strange information concerning McGovern. He'd described her as a friend and a "real looker," but more important perhaps, she was also a reporter. That made three reporters in the deck already, one of whom's press card was currently missing. I wasn't an enemy of the press, but when you're waiting for the cops to show up to install a trap and trace device to catch a kidnapper who soon might be calling, the last thing you need is some crusading media woman snooping around hoping to stick her proboscis into the sensitive spokes of your nightmare. I had to be careful, quick, and diplomatic.

"Hoover says you're a sexy little booger," I said, "but I'm pretty busy right now rearranging my traveling sock drawer and I—"

"I won't take up your valuable time," she said. "I just thought you'd be interested in what I've discovered about Mike McGovern. If you are, meet me tomorrow at the Bishop Museum right behind the display of the ancient outrigger canoe. I'll be there at three o'clock sharp."

"I can't promise—" I said, but Carline had hung up the phone.

By the time I'd cradled the blower, the cops were knocking on the door. A moment later they were in the room asking rudimentary questions, studying the ransom note, accepting my offer of coffee and poi rolls, and essentially waiting for the dicks and the techs to show up. When I asked if they thought they would be employing trap and trace techniques to catch the kidnappers they shrugged, demurred, and eventually asked if I thought room service had any *malasadas*. *Malasadas* are a popular Portuguese pastry at the islands. The hotel did not have any *malasadas*. They did have coffee and poi rolls. I ordered enough for a small bar mitzvah reception. Then I ventured another question.

"What are the odds," I asked, "I mean that all this is going to turn out okay?"

One of the uniforms simply shrugged again. The other one took a long look out to the sea and shook his head. His broad, dark face carried with it the ambivalent countenance of the people of Hawaii, ready to spontaneously break into a chant of joy or a song of sorrow.

"Too much *pilikia*," he said.

Pilikia, I later learned, is the Hawaiian word for trouble. I still don't know if the cop was referring to his life, his job, the world, saving McGovern, or all of the above. And now, of course, it'd probably be too much *pilikia* to find out.

Several pots of coffee and about nineteen poi rolls later, two dicks had arrived and were asking me a galaxy of questions and two techs were setting up their equipment on a table in the far corner of my hotel room. By the time the nascent dawn had spread its light across the land and the waters, we were more than ready to trap and trace. The two dicks were relaxing on the lanai, the techs had their headsets on, and I was taking a brief power nap when we caught our first fish.

"Wake up, Dickhead!" said Stephanie.

"Hello?"

"What's the matter? Are you *brain* dead? Are you in a fucking *coma?*"

With mounting irritation I could see the techs chuckling to each other. The conversation was also hooked up to some kind of speaker-phone so the two dicks had now come back into the room from the lanai with somewhat bemused expressions on their faces.

"Uh, Stephanie—"

"What happened? Your iron lung tilt over?"

All the cops were laughing now and I was becoming increasingly agitato, but at least I was fully awake.

"Listen, Stephanie, I don't have to take this shit. This call is being taped in order to trap and trace the kidnappers and—"

"I don't care if this call is being aired on *Hard Copy,* Dickhead. I'll trap your ass and trace my social security number on your balls!"

"Who's calling, please?"

"Admit it, Dickhead," said Stephanie, now clearly playing to the laughter that was very audible in the room. "You have to take any shit

I decide to give you because I'm five-foot-eleven and a half, more drop-dead gorgeous than Grace Kelly, smarter than you, funnier than you, richer than you, wiser than you—"

"But you don't like limericks—"

"I don't like *you*. What the hell's going on in your room, Parakeet Dick? It sounds like a meeting of the Gay Men's Breakfast Club."

The cops were now convulsing with laughter. I was sitting up in bed endeavoring to light my first cigar of the morning and scrambling what was left of my brains to find an effective ploy to get Stephanie off the phone.

"Listen, darling. It's important that we keep the line clear in case the people who are holding McGovern should call. Do you think we could take up these issues at another time? Or do I have to get a fork-lift in here and get you off the blower?"

"I can see you driving a forklift, Friedman. You'd probably kill yourself, which I wouldn't mind, but it would at least be the first job you've ever held in your life."

"Please hang up the phone, darling. We'll discuss all this later."

"Okay, Hebe. But don't forget you've been listening to your master's voice."

"Stephanie—"

"Don't *forget* it!" said Stephanie. "Ciao, Hebe."

She cradled the blower. I hung up as well. To my surprise there was light applause from the gathered multitudes in my hotel room.

"Jesus Christ," said one dick admiringly. "What a world-class ball-buster!"

"I wouldn't mind getting kidnapped by *that* broad," said the other dick.

I got out of bed and poured myself a cup of coffee. It's a strange mingling of emotions when you feel proud and ridiculous at the same time, but it's better than feeling nothing at all.

"Is she anything like what she sounds?" asked one of the techs, not impolitely.

I watched the birds on the lanai eating the poi rolls under the sign that read "Please Do Not Feed the Birds. *Mahalo*." I puffed my cigar and nodded thoughtfully.

"She's a whore with a heart of gold," I said.

Chapter Twenty-two

Blower traffic following Stephanie's little wake-up call was almost nonexistent that morning and it wasn't very long before one of the dicks and one of the techs drifted off. The remaining two cops assured me that everything was set up to trap and trace the kidnappers when and if they called. They would work in shifts, they said, and keep the operation going as long as it seemed feasible. I asked them how long that would be and they said it would be as long as the poi rolls and the coffee held out.

Around ten o'clock McCall popped by. He was wearing a bright aloha shirt, khaki shorts, Jesus boots, and mirrored sky-shooters, and he was carrying a medium-sized, seriously businesslike suitcase. He looked like a friendly, upscale dope dealer. I introduced him to the cops and he put the suitcase on the bed.

"It's all there," he said. "Fifty K in fives, tens, and twenties. All used bills."

"What took you so long?" I said. "You've probably got enough whip-out in your pocket to have made up most of it."

"Bankers are always bastards," said McCall. "And the smaller the transaction, the bigger the bastards they are. Now if this had been a really big ransom amount, say in the millions, I probably could've done the deal in a heartbeat."

"Maybe next time," said the cop, as he opened the suitcase and sorted through McCall's stash.

"They haven't called yet, have they?" asked McCall.

"No," I said. "The phones haven't exactly been ringing off the hook here at the Jerry Lewis Facial Tic Telethon."

"They'll call," said the dick grimly. "When they do, just remember what I told you. Agree to whatever they say, but take your time. The longer you keep 'em talking, the easier they are to trap and trace."

"What's trap and trace?" asked McCall, a moment or two later as the two of us sat on comfortable chairs on the lanai and tried to cipher the glittering ocean. The cops were still in the room recounting McCall's money.

"'Trap and trace,'" I said, "is the correct phrase for the modern police technique of tracing kidnappers' calls and shortly afterward, apprehending said kidnappers."

"Why don't they call it 'trace and trap'?" asked McCall.

"Why don't they call it 'roll 'n' rock'?" I said.

"Why don't we try to trap and trace some room service?" said the cop.

McCall ordered the Japanese Good Health Breakfast featuring seaweed, miso soup, and garlic fried rice. I ordered poi pancakes and a Spam omelette with Maui onions. The cop ordered a Portuguese sausage and two eggs sunny-side up. The tech said he'd stay with poi rolls and coffee. I also ordered another large pot of Kona coffee, a pitcher of ice water, and a pitcher of fresh guava juice.

"Whenever my father orders eggs sunny-side up," I said to the cop, "he always says, 'Give me two eggs looking at me.'"

"Your father's a smart man," said the cop. "You can't trust anybody these days."

The waiter was just removing the saran wrap condom from the pitcher of guava juice when the phones rang and everybody ran for his battle station. I ran for the blower by the bed, the tech ran for the table with all his equipment, the dick ran for the same locus I'd staked out for myself and lurked over my shoulder with a brisk, businesslike bedside manner, and the waiter ran for his life as McCall whipped out some whip-out and fat-armed him out the door into the hallway.

"Don't answer yet!" shouted the tech. "Let it ring a few more times."

Under the best of circumstances it's difficult for me to let a phone ring for very long. I'm an incurable blower addict who believes that every call contains within it the magical power to change my life. So far, of course, that call had never come. This time, however, I wasn't so sure that my life would stay the same. This could be the one I remember as clergymen are torturing me on my deathbed.

"Pick up *now!*" shouted the tech.

My adrenaline was red-lining and my hand was shakier than I'd wished as I hoisted the blower. As I said hello I saw McGovern's gentle, innocent face shimmering softly somewhere between the sunlight and the sea. This was a call that could change his life, too.

"Who's this?" said an emotionless voice.

"Kinky Friedman," I said.

"Well, Mr. Friedman," said the guy, with about as much feeling as somebody at the monthly meeting of a condo unit complaining about the landscaper's truck being parked in front of the building. "Do you have what we want?"

"I have it," I said.

McCall, who'd come back into the room quietly, stood by the door like a statue. The dick stood near the bed like a statue. Only the tech, listening in on his headset, nodded vague encouragement. Like Hank Williams, I felt so lonesome I could cry.

"Look out the window," said the voice on the blower.

A sudden chill went through me. If the guy could see me he could see there were other people in the room. If that were the case, it could be over already for McGovern. I looked out the window.

"You see the big old stone swimming pool that's built right out on the ocean?" He was referring to a structure called a natatorium, a World War I memorial that stood just down the beach from the hotel like an ancient ruin.

"I see it," I said.

"At eleven-thirty sharp be sitting on row thirteen of those stone bleachers inside that place. You can slip in by the hau tree through that old rusty gate on the Diamond Head side. And you better have what I want."

"Do you have what I want?" I said. "Can I speak to him?"

"Eleven-thirty. Row thirteen. If we see a single cop you'll never see your friend again. *Pau kanaka make.*"

The line went dead and the tech cursed and I cradled the blower. The dick looked over to the tech.

"Did you hook him?" he asked.

"Yeah," said the tech. "To a phone booth on Kapahulu."

"Shit," said the dick. "It's always a phone booth on Kapahulu."

"What does that tell us?" I asked.

"Not a fucking thing," said the dick.

"And what does *pau kanaka make* mean?"

"It means we better have your ass in row thirteen at eleven-thirty or your pal's worm-bait."

"Sounds better in Hawaiian," I said.

"Everything does," said the dick.

Chapter Twenty-three

Before I left the room with a suitcase full of cash, several other newly arrived dicks leaned on me to let one of their own stand in in my place. They reasoned, quite logically, that the kidnappers didn't know me from Adam and that an undercover in my stead might have a better chance of swapping the ransom for McGovern and coming out of the ordeal alive. I told them that there were already enough Kinky Friedman impersonators in the world and this was something that I had to do by myself. It was not necessarily rational but it was as personal as you could get. I also let the cops know that I didn't give a damn what my chances were of coming out alive if I couldn't drill a little hole and pull McGovern through with me. They said don't be a hero. Don't take chances. I told them Damon Runyon's great line: "All of life is six-to-five against." They said, fine. Let's send Damon Runyon. But that was all before I left the room with a suitcase full of cash.

There are many sobering experiences in life, but certainly not the least of them is setting out alone to trade ransom money with kidnappers for the life of your favorite Irish poet. Love and money were hanging in the balance as I ankled it out of the hotel lobby like a tourist traveling light. I skirted the beach and legged it through a shady hau tree canopy. It was almost eleven o'clock in the morning in Honolulu, but a chill was knifing through me deeper than childhood. Its name was *pau kanaka make*.

The "big old stone swimming pool" that the kidnappers had chosen as the rendezvous point was actually an Olympic-sized, saltwater pool called a natatorium. It had been built right after World War I as a memorial to all the flesh and blood toy soldiers the child of man had swept off the table long ago and far away. Now it stood before me in all its faded glory, the edifice crumbling slowly like my confidence in the success of the transaction about to occur within its weather-beaten walls.

The choice of the natatorium demonstrated some degree of canniness on the part of the kidnappers, since it stood solitary and aloof like a goddess of liberty beside a teeming shore. Glimpsing the stone bleachers inside the walls was almost as difficult as glimpsing the former glory of the place. But I could feel the ambience of the past all around me as I snaked my way through sea sponges and beer cans and all the detritus of modern life up to the rusted gates of yesterday's Eden. Just as the man on the phone had said, the gate was partially open and it wasn't difficult for me to worm my way into the empty ruin. The only witness observing my entrance, as far as I could tell, was a longhaired, orange-colored cat with large yellow eyes that seemed to reflect my own distrust of the whole damn world in general and this situation in particular. The cat, I noticed, had the good sense not to enter the natatorium.

"I *am* Bozo the Clown," I said to the cat, as I left the sunlight behind and walked warily into a dank, darkened hallway. Maybe, I thought, it had been a mistake not to let an undercover dick handle the ransom exchange. Maybe I should've pressed the cops further regarding their plan of action or what I should do if anything went wrong. There was a lot of room for something to go wrong, I reflected, as I lost sight of the carefree, civilized world and wandered my way gingerly through the shadowy bowels of the natatorium. The cops had outfitted me with a Kel transmitter, but they'd warned that it didn't always work well in urban areas. I didn't know if the archaeological ruin I was currently inhabiting qualified as an urban area or not, but unless the cops had scuba divers in the pool or a submarine with a periscope, they were going to have a hell of a time monitoring whatever was about to happen. This was not particularly heartening news for the Kinkster.

I sloshed through the stagnant water of the tunnel for about seven years and at last emerged into the bright sunlight at poolside. I walked up the stone mountain with the suitcase to row thirteen and sat down facing the pool and then the sea. The tourists on the beach were now far away in my distant peripheral vision. Not a living soul stirred within the confines of my castle. A soft breeze blew in ghostlike from the direction of Diamond Head. It was five to eleven. I sat back in the sun and waited for the show.

If I'd been around in the Roaring Twenties the place would've been packed. The great Duke Kahanamoku took the first official swim here in 1927, emerging from the water to a raucous ovation. Johnny Weissmuller competed here as well, along with Buster Crabbe, who later replaced him in the *Tarzan* movies. They swim in the skies now and the decrepit lonely pool pouted like a long-lost lover; the fame, the glory, the happy tanned faces of the cheering crowds all had faded forever like a coda to the Jazz Age. The kidnappers were late. I couldn't stand kidnappers who were late.

"We'll take that suitcase now," said a voice behind me that almost made me jump through my asshole for America. Grabbing the suitcase tightly, I turned around to confront two men who'd materialized from a small alcove at the top of the stone bleachers. They wore aloha shirts, jeans, and tennis shoes and their demeanor was casual, confident, and almost ruthlessly positive, like they were picking up a suitcase for Christ.

"Hold the weddin'," I said. "Where's McGovern?"

"Listen close, cuz," said one of the men. "Here's how it works. You hand over the suitcase. I punch in some numbers on this cell phone. I tell 'em the money's here. They cut your friend loose."

"How about we reach out and touch someone first?" I said. "How about you punch some numbers on that cell phone and you let me hear McGovern's voice so I know he's okay?"

"How about you give me that suitcase," said the guy, "before I blow your fucking head off?"

It's never very polite to point a gun at anyone, and if you've ever had anybody do it to you, you know how it feels. It didn't require a lot of imagination to visualize these guys blowing away a lonely haole in a deserted natatorium, grabbing the suitcase full of money, and heading to the Disneyland of their choosing. The only question in my mind was whether they'd leave the body on the stone bleachers in the sun for the seabirds to peck out the eyes or whether they'd throw it in the pool that, because of structural deterioration, mingled with the seawater just enough to allow tiny fishes to swim in and dart up the flaccid penis of the corpse. While both were attractive scenarios, I felt it was time to head for the exits, which unfortunately had not been clearly marked for over seventy years. As I stumbled over a paving stone and went flying, two shouts and a shot rang out, reverberating through the empty natatorium like a little drummer boy marching along the synapses of my nervous system. The shot missed but ricocheted unpleasantly close to my left ear. The two shouts sounded something like this: "Drop that suitcase, motherfucker!" and, "Freeze! Police!"

By the time I'd picked myself up from row seven, the cops had moved in and collared the two kidnappers. The same dick who'd been in the hotel room came over and coolly assessed my well-being and the well-being of the suitcase. We were both a little scuffed up but apparently we passed his inspection.

"We know these guys," said the cop. "They're local scammers. The gang who couldn't shoot straight."

"Now you tell me," I said, more heartbroken than I wanted him to know.

"The point is they don't have your friend," said the cop. "They couldn't successfully kidnap a tame mongoose."

"So who *is* holding McGovern?" I said. The cop didn't answer. He just shrugged and turned and looked out over the endless, blue, billowing blanket of the sea.

PART FIVE

On the Nod

Chapter Twenty-four

The ship of fools was lurching out of control. Maybe it had never been in control. All I knew now that I didn't know before I'd come to Hawaii was that man could not live on poi rolls alone. McGovern was not in the morgue, not in the mental hospital, and he hadn't been kidnapped by the local gang of scam artists who'd sent us the ransom note. That left a worldful of tragic possibilities, almost none of which I wished to dwell on very long. The unaimed arrow that the Hawaiians often speak of was probably still whizzing around somewhere and I was becoming sadly resigned to the fact that its target was going to be either my ass as a detective or my heart as a friend.

"Every lead we follow seems to be taking us nowhere," I remarked to Hoover as we drove along the highway toward the Bishop Museum that afternoon. "It's really quite disheartening."

"Kind of like trying to write a limerick," said Hoover. "I've been working on one for the past three days and the damn thing just won't resolve itself."

"Keep working," I said, "but keep it to yourself. When it's finished I'm sure Stephanie will enjoy hearing you recite it. She admires your work."

"I admire her tits," said Hoover. "Maybe I should write one about her tits."

"She'd love it."

"You know, I've been thinking. Detectives aren't the only ones who follow leads. Reporters also follow leads. After all, McGovern himself was a reporter."

"What do you mean *was* a reporter?"

"Just what I said. You've got to be realistic about this, Kinkyhead. The guy's been missing a week. He's got to know people are worried as shit. He's got to figure his friends are desperately looking for him. If he hasn't contacted us what else could it mean?"

"'MIT!—MIT!—MIT!'" I said.

"You already told me about that Man in Trouble Hot Line business. But you got that call when you were still back in New York. Neither you nor anyone else we know has heard a word from McGovern since. What does that tell you?"

I puffed desultorily on my cigar and watched the palm trees fly by through the window. They say the truth can set you free, but it can also break your heart.

"You've got to look at this with a reporter's eye," Hoover continued relentlessly. "You've been searching for clues and patterns too much. Just try covering the story for a while."

"Just try driving your vehicle," I said, as Hoover narrowly missed a pickup truck loaded with pineapples.

"What I'm saying is this Carline woman has a great nose for a story. She also has some other obvious physical assets that will become apparent to you when you meet her. The point is she wouldn't tell you she's got some possible information on McGovern and go to the trouble of arranging this meeting with us at the Bishop Museum unless she's stumbled onto something pretty damn significant. So don't give up hope."

"I haven't," I said. "But mere moments ago you were speaking of McGovern in the past tense."

"Anything's possible," said Hoover. "For three days they spoke of Jesus Christ in the past tense, too."

"What is this? Vacation Bible Class?"

"Then, of course, He came back to life on Groundhog Day," said Hoover.

Hoover kept driving. I kept trying to look at things through a reporter's eye. I found myself wondering what would happen if a man with a reporter's eye met a woman with a nose for a story. Would Mc-Govern magically materialize?

"Why do we have to meet this broad at the Bishop Museum?" I asked Hoover, as he continued undaunted on our cross-island odyssey.

"I don't know exactly why," said Hoover. "I just know that the Bishop Museum is an important place to both Carline and myself. It's not only the most authentic and comprehensive museum in all Polynesia, but it's also the place from which Carline and I have gotten a lot of material. That's where I first broke the story on the *ka'ai*."

"What the hell is a *ka'ai*?"

"First of all, they're plural. There are two of them. Woven baskets bearing the bones of ancient kings. Second of all, they're the two oldest relics in Hawaiian culture—"

"And I thought *we* were."

"And third of all, the *ka'ai* were stolen five years ago from the Bishop Museum and they're still missing."

"So's McGovern," I said.

Chapter Twenty-five

The Bishop Museum turned out to be a Gothic three-story, mildly foreboding, castlelike structure that you wouldn't want to wander around in after dark. Obviously, somebody had, or the *ka'ai*, of which Hoover had spoken, would not have been missing. If they were gone, however, just about everything else remotely representative of Hawaii was still on display. Indeed, like any museum worth the name, the Bishop Museum was more than anything else the attic of the land it loved. It stood as a proud shrine beckoning you forward if you believed in yesterday.

As Hoover and I stood on the third-floor landing waiting for his friend Carline and studying the fifty-foot-long stuffed sperm whale, I realized not for the first time how terribly drawn I was to death-bound people. All people are death-bound, of course, but some of us seem to be riding a faster train, and these charm-laden individuals appear to luxuriate with life in such fashion as to draw me to them like a moth to the ragged flame of friendship. Many of the most charismatic people I'd known in my life had already prematurely ejaculated and gone to Jesus. The list was unnaturally long, but the ones I lamped on while communing with the sperm whale were my brother Tom Baker, John Belushi, Lowell George, Keith Moon, and Abbie Hoffman. All of them seemed, in memory, to have Anne Frank's eyes. Even the sperm whale seemed to have Anne Frank's eyes. Maybe it was merely the dead telling the living that it was all right.

Though it was possibly too late already, I did not want McGovern to be one of the dead people in my little black telephone book. I thought that maybe if I didn't glamorize or lionize him it might sustain his presence somehow on this wretched excuse for a planet. There was nothing to it of course. No logic whatsoever. I just figured if I really started missing him he'd probably be gone. So I stared into one of the huge glass eyes of the sperm whale and tried to remember a few things that really irritated me about McGovern. It wasn't too difficult.

One of the most maddening aspects of any form of interpersonal relations with McGovern was the absolutely unavoidable experience of exposing oneself to the legendary living-room tape he'd put together of some of his favorite artists. Everywhere McGovern traveled on this green earth he took the tape with him and played it endlessly, ruthlessly, relentlessly, brutally, until his companions of the moment begged to be taken immediately to the nearest mental hospital.

The tape itself, if you only heard it once or twice, wasn't bad, and even demonstrated a bit of McGovern's soulfulness, as well as his diversity, though it did tend to lean rather heavily toward the kind of music that was undoubtedly accompanied in McGovern's brain by the sounds of ballroom skirts rustling across long-ago dance floors. The tape started with Nilsson singing the old Fred Neil song "Everybody's Talkin'," and then, in a random and haphazard order, went on to Bessie Smith, Frank Sinatra, Duke Ellington, "The Girl from Ipanema," "Swing, Swing, Swing" by Benny Goodman, Van Morrison, Stephane Grappelli, "Back Door Man" by Willie Dixon, and a number of other tunes I've understandably repressed because I've heard the cursed tape about seven million times. There is nothing wrong with the individual artists or the individual songs, but there is something about this material, when taken together as an aggregate and forced upon you constantly, seductively, subliminally, that will make you start to think like McGovern and drink like McGovern and I'm not sure which is worse.

Some years back I had traveled with McCall on his jet to a sunny couple of weeks in a mansion overlooking the sea at Cabo San Lucas. The entourage had included McGovern, my sister Marcie, Russell Walker (McCall's right- and left-hand man), several lesbians, and several heterosexuals who may be shy about seeing their names in print.

McGovern was certainly not shy about throwing his tape on the sound system of the giant house as soon as we'd gotten there. A few days later, some of the group had come down with food poisoning, including McGovern. When I hadn't noticed him come out of his room for some time I started seriously worrying about his health.

"Do you think McGovern has passed away?" I asked Marcie that afternoon as we sat in deck chairs beside the pool.

"Of course he's alive," she said. "His fucking tape is playing."

More recently, on a trip to McCall's place in La Jolla, McCall had mocked McGovern's tape and I had been uncharacteristically critical of both the tape in particular and McGovern in general. I called repeatedly for the sounds of silence in the house and at last McGovern had yielded to the pressure and turned off the tape. I was dimly aware that the songs were of a deep personal nature and an undoubtedly meditational value to McGovern, yet I continued to cast asparagus upon McGovern and his music. Certainly he was aware, I contended, that the constant playing of his homemade tape drove any sentient being, including myself, half-crazy. Yet the big man did not rise to his own defense. He did not even appear to be angry. He held the little cassette stoically, lovingly, in his big hand.

"I just want to go someplace," said McGovern, "where people appreciate my tape."

As tiresome as I sometimes found McGovern, I very much hoped that on some sunny isle somewhere his tape was playing. Maybe it was playing on some isolated, seldom-visited, beautiful beach on the very isle upon which I stood next to my pal Hoover waiting for his friend Carline, watching the carnival-mirror-eye of a sad, stuffed sperm whale speaking with the voice of Earl Buckelew saying that everything will come out in the wash if you use enough Tide, only the sperm whale was no doubt referring to something other than the well-known household detergent.

"Carline's usually very punctual," said Hoover. "I've never known her to be this late."

"Maybe she can't swallow the idea of this sperm whale," I said.

Chapter Twenty-six

"This is some strange shit," said Hoover about twenty minutes later as we stood in front of a full-length red-and-yellow feather cloak.

"It says here," I said, "that less than a hundred of these feather garments are extant in the world today. The shy o-o bird contributed the yellow feather on the underside of each wing. Unfortunately, the o-o is not extant today. Now the red feathers, it claims here—"

"I wasn't talking about the fucking cloak," said Hoover. "I was commenting on the strange fact that Carline isn't here to meet us. I've worked with her for six years. I know her habits and her ways. She's not a frivolous sort. If Carline says it's important, it's important. And she's a real stickler about meetings. If Carline says she'll be here, she'll be here. Something is definitely not kosher."

"An unfortunate choice of words," I said, as I continued to study the last masterpiece of the o-o bird. "What makes you so sure this flaky broad could shed some light on McGovern anyway?"

Hoover stared at me in disbelief. I continued to stare at the feathered cloak. The reds and yellows seemed so vivid and velvety, so vital that it wouldn't have surprised me terribly if the damned thing lifted off and flew out the window of the museum. It was truly remarkable how intricately the patterns of colors had been attached to the base of fiber netting. The reds and the yellows flowed delicately together like the winding rivers of our lives.

"She's not a flaky broad," said Hoover.

"Who's not a flaky broad?"

"Aha, Kinkyhead! Like Captain Cook before you you've succumbed to the magic of the feather cloak."

"Hardly, Watson, hardly. I am merely observing the vital beauty of its plumage."

"And what do your observational powers tell you, Holmes?"

"They tell me that if somebody tickled your ass with a feather, this cloak could probably send your penis to Venus."

"You stay right here and commune with your feathered friend and I'm going to find a phone and try to find Carline. I can't believe she stood us up like this."

"This feather cloak is amazing," I said. "It's more alive than most people I know."

By the time I turned around, Hoover was no longer there. A brilliant red-and-yellow kaleidoscopic after-image was swimming before my eyes. The colors seemed to pulse with life, almost as if they were trying to tell me something. I was beginning to wish that somebody would tell me something soon, because if the search for McGovern were to drag on much longer with no solid leads, I'd no doubt be ready to resign from the human race.

I'd been prepared, of course, for the blind alleys, cul-de-sacs, bogus kidnappings, and mental hospital field trips that invariably become part of any investigator's life. But I hadn't counted on the case trying my talents and my tenderness quite as ruthlessly as it had thus far. Wandering around the museum like a Jewish mariachi, I sadly realized once again how very little light had truly been shed upon the case since I'd left the island of Manhattan for the island of Oahu. A woman had apparently lured McGovern from the beach that fateful night at Waikiki. Now another woman, apparently, had some information regarding McGovern that she wished to impart to me. Unfortunately, she did not seem to place a high priority in keeping her appointments. It wasn't, I thought, a hell of a lot to show for my efforts. In detective work, however, what you're able to rule out can sometimes be as important as what you're able to rule in, especially if you know how to bend the rules.

"That's fucking great," Hoover was mumbling to himself as he came back into the room. "Carline didn't file her stories this morning at the *Advertiser*."

"And?"

"And it's the first time she's missed a deadline in six years."

"Nobody's perfect," I said, as I examined an empty glass exhibition case. "What's this empty glass cabinet supposed to signify?"

"It signifies that while nobody's perfect you're being a perfect asshole not to be concerned that something may have happened to my friend Carline who was trying to help you find McGovern. The exhibit case is also where the *ka'ai* used to be. If you look carefully you'll notice that they're missing. Like McGovern. And now Carline."

"Hold the weddin'," I said. "I don't care about these fucking *ka'ai*—"

"Keep your voice down. They're the most sacred relics in the history of Hawaii."

"—but I think it's a stretch to say that Carline's missing just because she didn't show up for a fucking appointment!"

A large woman in a purple muumuu glared malevolently at me from across the room. Whether she was concerned about the history of Hawaii or the language of the Kinkster I couldn't say for certain. Other visitors to the museum appeared to be staring at us now as well. Some had small children in hand and eyes filled with righteous indignation. Clearly, the nonmeeting with Carline here at the museum had been about as helpful to the investigation as the phony ransom demand earlier in the day. Clearly, my frustration with the lack of progress in the case had begun to affect my rational thought processes and my usual Gandhi-like spirit. Clearly, it was time to leave the Bishop Museum.

Sooner or later, I figured, things had to come to a head. As if the old Hawaiian gods were with us, we stumbled upon one as we were beating a hasty exit from a roomful of ancient relics and irritated tourists. Hoover was the one who saw it first.

"Goddamn, Kinkyhead!" he ejaculated. "Look at *this* head!"

I glanced at the full-size, sculpted wooden head and almost did a Danny Thomas coffee spit without the coffee. As I took a closer look, spiky little sea creatures seemed to be crawling up my spine.

"Mother of God!" I said. "It's uncanny!"

"It's more than uncanny," said Hoover. "It's virtually goddamn impossible. That bust looks like it's been gathering dust here forever. It's got to be centuries old."

"It can't be."

"It can't be but it damn sure is."

"Curiouser and curiouser," I said, as I stared into the eyes of the mute, brown wooden relic, while Hoover made copious notes in his little reporter's notebook recording the interminably long name of the ancient high chief and the scant biographical data the museum had provided.

"Where are you?" I said to the brown wooden head.

This was not as inane a question as it might've seemed. The bust was incredibly, insanely, undeniably, a dead ringer for McGovern.

Chapter Twenty-seven

"We've got to find Carline," I said, as Hoover's little car sped past a breathtaking panorama of palm trees, white beaches, and the lonely, lovely aquamarine sea. Quite understandably, neither of us was very big on the scenery at the moment.

"I'm glad you're finally coming around to my viewpoint, Sherlock. Two people have disappeared now and I'm sure what they have in common has occurred to you. They're both reporters."

"Clever, Watson. Very clever. If God is in His heavens, the next one to disappear will be you."

For the next few minutes we proceeded toward the hotel in a rather sullen silence. My mind was furiously connecting the dots along a distant shoreline when Hoover piped up again.

"Seriously, Sherlock," he said, "you must've come up with some explanation for the fact that McGovern is the spitting image of some chief who died many hundreds of years ago."

"The only theory I've posited at this time will not be much help to us. I've determined that the older the chief, the longer the name. What's your theory, Watson?"

"It probably won't help us much either. My theory is if men could blow their own dicks, the human race would cease to exist."

"Insightful, Watson. Very insightful. I don't suppose in all your frantic scrawlings at the museum you were able to record the interminably long name of the ancient chief?"

"Hey. I'm a reporter. When I cover a story it damn well gets its ass covered, Kinkyhead."

"Perhaps you'd like to share it with the rest of the class. In the hastiness of our departure from the museum, and without my reading skepticals, I failed to observe all the small print."

As he drove precariously along the edge of a pali, Hoover gamely endeavored to extract his notebook from his pocket and to locate his notes in that aforementioned little book. These activities were not brick and mortar to feelings of confidence and well-being on the part of Hoover's passenger.

"Well, let's see," Hoover was saying. "McGovern's great-great-great-great-great-great-grandfather apparently lived around the fifteenth or sixteenth centuries. Give or take a few hundred years. His real skull is hidden inside one of the *ka'ai*, which I know you're eager to hear about and of course, like the *ka'ai*, the skull is missing."

"I'm becoming more interested in the *ka'ai* all the time. What else?"

"This guy who looked like McGovern's twin brother was evidently the great-grandson of Liloa, whoever the hell *he* was."

In my mind pieces were now falling together in fond, familiar fashion. I wasn't sure if Hoover's friend Carline Ravel was really missing or if she'd just come up with a hotter date than meeting two geezers at a museum. It had, of course, been her idea to meet there, which, I supposed, suggested something. Precisely what it suggested I wasn't precisely sure. All I felt for certain was that these were deeper waters than even the mighty Pacific. They were far too deep, I now believed, for McGovern ever to have drowned in them.

"Obviously," I said, "this guy Liloa must've been very important in his day. Now two men are driving across the island in a beat-up Mazda on our way to the hotel and we never heard of him. That doesn't say much for fame and immortality."

"Don't tell me about fame and immortality," said Hoover. "I remember years ago back in Nashville when John Hartford had the big hit with 'Gentle on My Mind.' I also had an album out at the time that included the song 'Sometimes That's All That Keeps You Goin'.'"

"Great song. I remember it."

"Don't put me up on a pedestal now. Anyway, I was friends with

Hartford and he and I were both published and produced by the Glaser Brothers, so we went out on the road together with me opening some shows for him. When the tour started out John made a big deal of introducing me to all the reporters. He'd say, 'This is my friend Will Hoover. He's a brilliant songwriter and he's got this great new album, which you've got to listen to. Hoover's going to be a big star,' and so on and so on.

"It was very gracious of Hartford to do that, but then 'Gentle On My Mind' started to become a really monster hit. I noticed that in each successive town we played, John's introduction of me to the press became increasingly attenuated, until one night—I believe it was in Atlanta—he hadn't bothered to introduce me at all. One of the reporters finally gestured in my direction and asked him, 'Who's that guy standing over there in the dressing room?' Hartford told him: 'He's the boy who travels with me.'"

"That's a great line. But your devolution with John Hartford occurred over a period of weeks or months. It took a couple of culture-bound idiots like ourselves many centuries to be ignorant of Liloa's talents. But he was only the great-grandfather, you say, of the man whose carved wooden head now resides in the Bishop Museum just waiting to make hapless friends of McGovern jump through their assholes. To hell with the great-grandfather! Who was the actual Mike McGovern impersonator?"

"Well, let's see. He was a high chief, of course. That's why they put his skull and his bones inside one of the *ka'ai*—"

"The fucking *ka'ai* again—"

"Which *are* Hawaii's most sacred relics—"

"What was his *name?*"

"I know I've got it here somewhere. I wrote it down. It's a long fucker."

"Not as long as the John Hartford story."

"Here it is," said Hoover. "But I can't quite make out my writing."

"Try making out the line in the middle of the road," I said irritably. "Try making out the vehicle in front of us. The last thing we need is for you to rear-end some guy and then we'd have to get a charge of sodomy reduced to following too closely. Why don't you just pull over?"

"Because we're almost at the goddamn hotel."

"Watch it!"

"I saw them."

"It's not often when you have the opportunity to run over three generations of tourists from Iowa."

"*I'm* from Iowa," said Hoover somewhat defensively. "Why do you always have to pick on Iowa?"

"Okay, Indiana," I said. "Is that better?"

"Damn straight," said Hoover, taking out his notebook and steering precariously with one hand while glancing quickly back and forth between the book and the road. "If they were only from Indiana I'm going to try to read this guy's name again."

"God help us."

"He wasn't a god. He was a high chief. And his name was— Lonoikamakahiki!"

"That *is* a long booger. Jesus Christ!"

"Was He a god or a high chief?"

"Say that name again."

"You mean Lonoikamakahiki?" said Hoover. "That was pretty smooth pronunciation for a haole from Iowa. Of course I *have* lived here ten years—"

But I was no longer listening to Hoover. I was listening to a phone call I'd gotten over a week ago just before I'd left New York. As I listened to the wires humming a cold curtain of certainty came down somewhere inside my fevered brain.

"'Hang loose,'" I said. "'Lono is home.'"

Chapter Twenty-eight

"So, Dickhead," said Stephanie, "you think it's the same Lono?"

"I'd bet McGovern's life on it," I said.

It was later that evening and the two of us were eating Hong Kong roast chicken and steamed flounder at Wong & Wong's Restaurant in Chinatown. Hoover was due to meet us shortly with an update on the Carline situation. McCall was following up on some additional FBI leads that Russell Walker had turned up on McGovern. I wasn't holding my breath.

"The Lono connection is something at least," I said. "It's somewhere to start when Rambam gets out here."

"Oh, great," said Stephanie. "That's all we need. A pompous, macho P. I. running around in a Speedo with a satellite dish on his head."

"Rambam wouldn't be caught dead in a Speedo. And he only wears the satellite dish on his head for very important cases."

"Let's go over what we have," said Stephanie with her usual lawyerly, methodical approach to things, "before Rambam blows in and fucks everything up. We know the ransom attempt on McGovern was bogus. There's a carved wooden head in some museum of some ancient high chief that you and Hoover think looks like McGovern—"

"I'm telling you it's his identical twin. It's so similar it's spooky. If you don't believe me go down to the Bishop Museum and look at the head."

"It's bad enough I have to look at your head. Now where were we.

The kidnapping was bogus. The head looks like McGovern. The phone call said 'Lono is home.' And the head is a likeness of an ancient Hawaiian high chief named—"

"Lonoikamakahiki."

"Lonoikamakahiki?"

"Hey!" I said. "That's pretty good for a shiksa."

"And you think it's the same Lono?"

"I'd bet McGovern's life on it."

"You're starting to repeat yourself. You go into a brain-dead state after two piña coladas. How are you ever going to solve this case?"

"By figuring out where Lono's home is and discovering who knew that Mike McGovern was the spitting image of Lono."

"You can't build a case on superstition and coincidence, asshole. There's no rational thought process or deductive reasoning happening there. The reality is that not only is McGovern still missing in action, but Hoover's friend has also now apparently disappeared. Aren't you concerned about that? Have you even figured out that both the victims are reporters?"

"Sure. And I bet the culprit is an overbearing editor. No, Watson, what we're dealing with here goes beyond the boundaries of mere rational thought. You must suspend your tidy, anal-neurotic, culture-bound credibility and allow your outrigger to drift into the deep, mystical waters in the world of the kahuna. The unaimed arrow never misses."

"What a joke."

"You don't believe the unaimed arrow never misses?"

"Unless the target is your dick."

"Now that you mention it, I have noticed the recent rather disturbing development upon my person of a small scrotal wart."

"I'll never see it," said Stephanie, "unless I have to identify your body."

"Well, it's a small thing really. But the investigation seems to have expanded. Unless this lady reporter checks in very soon with Hoover or her boss at the *Advertiser,* we may assume that we're now searching for two missing parties instead of one."

"You're a fucking genius, Friedman. Did anyone ever tell you that?"

"People have been telling me that my whole miserable life."

"Well, they've been badly misleading you. You *still* don't have a clue as to McGovern's condition or his whereabouts and now you'll probably be spinning more of the few wheels that you have left in your brain looking for this woman when her disappearance may or may *not* be related to McGovern's."

"Of course it's related. Why do you think she was trying to arrange a meeting with us at the museum?"

"Because of the head?"

"Because of the head. Speaking of which, I wonder if they have a dumper in this place."

As I wandered through the back of Wong & Wong's I was impressed again with how similar it looked and felt to Big Wong's in New York. Both had killer-bee food and both were fraught with adventures for anyone attempting to navigate his or her way to his or her dumper. It was just possible that one of the Wongs of Wong & Wong's was related to the Wong of Big Wong's in some fashion. I'd have to inquire about it sometime when I didn't have so much on my plate.

After successfully grabbing a Republican by the neck, I washed my hands in the old tin sink and glanced in the slightly silvered men's room mirror. Something in the irregular blotched and burnished quality of that particular plane reminded me of a man looking out to sea. The man looking back at me, indubitably, was already half-past out to sea. There was, I reckoned, a timeless evil of some nature being perpetrated by the forces that seduced my friend McGovern to Hawaii with the free ticket that had disappeared along with that large American.

There was an insidious plan here that went beyond ransom money or mere foul play. I had to conclude that Hoover and I, and very probably Carline, were not the first to have tumbled upon McGovern's uncanny resemblance to Lono. This, if true, limited the field considerably. It meant that someone of the precious few on the planet who knew what Lono looked like also had known McGovern by sight. Manhattan and Oahu were not neighboring islands. Lono's bust was covered with dust. In all his years with the *Daily News* I'd never known McGovern's picture to be displayed beside his byline. A person who might've seen them both had to be rarer than the o-o bird.

There was turmoil and confusion beneath the surface of the face in the mirror. The eyes of my reflection would not quite meet my own. Should I apply Sherlockian dictum to the situation? Should I rely upon the path of the unaimed arrow of the mystical kahuna? Should I attempt to hang myself whilst masturbating in a cheap, tawdry, rather transparent effort to get Stephanie's attention? Should I go back to New York empty-handed and broken-hearted? Should I go back to the days before Damien, Duke, and Don Ho? Should I go back to the table?

When I did I noticed that another guy was sitting in my chair puffing on a cigar and conversing with Stephanie. At first I thought it was me but the two of them seemed to be getting along too amiably. When I got a little closer I realized it was Will Hoover. Neither he nor Stephanie appeared eager to welcome my return from the dumper. Indeed, they appeared locked in a rather highly animated rictus of dialogue.

"I'll take the Jesus seat," I said, pulling up a chair from another table and sitting at a position equidistant from the two of them. Neither appeared to notice.

"As a world-class ball-buster myself," Stephanie was saying with some little pride, "I know better than anyone else when Friedman is whipped. He doesn't have a clue except for that fucking head. God created the whole world in less time than it takes Friedman to find the men's room."

"He has had a few penis coladas," said Hoover.

"He never could hold his liquor," said Stephanie. "And that wasn't even remotely funny."

"I still think ol' Kinkyhead's going to pull this one out," maintained Hoover stalwartly.

"Pull it out?" shrieked Stephanie. "He can't even pull his own head out of his own ass. The only thing he's liable to pull out is his pathetic dick on the beach one day and get himself arrested for exposure."

"With a huge shlong like mine," I said, "I could die of exposure."

Indeed, it seemed as if I'd already died and gone to heaven because neither of my companions appeared to be acknowledging my presence at the table. Hoover, totally oblivious to me, continued his bold defense of the Kinkster's crime-solving capabilities.

"I even told Carline," he said, "a long time before all this started. I told her, and I wasn't bullshitting, that Kinky has solved every single goddamn investigation he's ever tackled. And that's the truth. I never realized when I told her, of course, that her very life might depend on his talents."

"He hasn't found McGovern," said Stephanie stubbornly. "How do you expect him to find your friend?"

"When I find McGovern I'll find Carline," I said.

"People's *lives* are at stake, Dickhead," said Stephanie. "This isn't like finding your cigar-cutter or finding a parking place. Oh, I for*got. You* don't drive."

"I *do* drive," I said. "I just don't drive in large, unfamiliar cities. But when I *am* driving and I'm looking for a parking place I always say: 'Hail, Mary, full of grace. Help me find a parking place.' And I always find one."

"What a joke," said Stephanie.

"Well, this isn't getting us anywhere," said Hoover. "I do have a rather strange document concerning the *ka'ai* that Carline left in my safekeeping some time ago. It's only a handful of pages long but I haven't deeply perused it for reasons that will soon become obvious."

"What's a *ka'ai*?" asked Stephanie.

"Hoover has a clinical recall on the subject," I said. "I'm sure he'll tell you all about it."

Hoover ran true to form. He warmed to the task as he went along, making a little show of polishing his glasses and reading from a prepared statement like a press secretary.

"'*Ka'ai*: sennit basketry caskets containing the bones of deified chiefs. *Ka'ai* Number One: braided and woven casket of coconut-husk fiber in the form of a human figure. A circular piece is sewed to the front of the torso. *Ka'ai* Number Two: braided and woven casket of coconut-husk fiber in the form of a human figure. The left eye is represented by a pearl shell. It is impossible to positively identify the remains encased in the two plaited sennit bone containers. Their alleged association is with fifteenth- or sixteenth-century high chiefs Liloa and Lonoikamakahiki.' Are you still with me?"

"Friedman's gone into a coma," said Stephanie, "but I think it's fascinating."

"'The *ka'ai* are said to have come from the mausoleum of Hale o Keawe at Honauna or Hale o Liloa in Waipi'o Valley. They were moved in 1858 to the Royal Tomb at Pohukinia on the grounds of Iolani Palace in Honolulu—'"

"Which had electricity four years before the White House," I said.

"Stop interrupting, asshole," said Stephanie.

"'—and from there to the Royal Mausoleum at Mauna 'Ala in Nu'uanu Valley in 1865. On March 15, 1918, Bishop Museum received the *ka'ai*. On February 24, 1994, at 1:15 in the afternoon they were discovered missing by the staff, police were notified, and the investigation began.'"

"And they still haven't found them?" asked Stephanie.

"That's right. Carline Ravel covered almost every step of the investigation. It's a little ironic that she should now disappear herself."

"Ironic is not quite the word I would've used," I said.

"Kinkyhead's onto something," said Hoover. "I can always tell."

"The only bones Friedman would like to be onto," said Stephanie, "are mine. And that'll never happen."

"Never say never," I said.

"Never!" said Stephanie, but she gave me such a stunner of a mischievous smile that the thing with feathers almost fell off of my soul.

"Anyway," said Hoover, "here's the strange little document I told you about that Carline left in my care." He handed me a small sheaf of papers stapled together at one corner.

"When did she give you this?" I said.

"I don't know," said Hoover. "Maybe five or six years ago."

"And you say you've never deeply perused it?"

"I'm not as crazy as I look," said Hoover. "Read the cover page."

In the bright lights of Wong & Wong's Restaurant I dutifully read Carline Ravel's short, handwritten cover letter. As I studied the note, little sea urchins began to crawl up the back of my neck. It read as follows:

"Caution. These pages include the never-published, little-known X-rays of the sacred *ka'ai*. There are those who believe it is a curse even to view them. The *ka'ai* being the most revered and sacred of all Hawaiian relics, the reader is requested to consider the advisability of proceeding further. The X-rays were made in 1919. No one involved is still living."

"I eyeballed them just a moment ago," said Hoover, "and already I have a hangnail."

Chapter Twenty-nine

It's always a pretty good idea never to put too much stock in the dreams you dream while you're sleeping. Scientists now know that these dreams are caused by gas, the same natural phenomenon that causes indigestion, makes a baby smile, or, when in large supply, can lend a harsh and unsavory note to somebody's elegant, tastefully planned dinner party. Dreams may seem wondrous or they may seem terrible, but they signify absolutely nothing except a possible early warning sign that the dreamer may be about to blast off for the nearest space station, which, if not unmanned, certainly will be when the dreamer arrives.

All this having been said, there are yet those superstitious souls amongst us who believe that the gas may be trying to tell us something. We don't believe in God and we don't believe in dreams; we just believe that nothing, not even life itself, can possibly be as meaningless as it usually seems. This is the sort of perverse, nihilistic thinking that can propel even a well-meaning person into becoming that most despised form of sentient life on the planet, an optimist. As a child the optimist unwraps a Christmas present, finds out it's a large box of horseshit, and says, "Somewhere there's got to be a pony." As an adult the optimist has long ago learned that there is no pony, just miles and miles of bathroom tiles, each one covered with a thin veneer of horseshit and wild honey and the poor bastard still thinks it might be appropriate to kill a large number of trees so idiots like myself can projectile-vomit onto the page the kind of prose that, come to think of it, is probably also caused by gas. Personally, I've never been stupid enough to be an optimist. I know things are going to turn out shitty, but I've got my mind set to enjoy it. If you're perverse enough you might just be able to pull it off. And the good news is it's the kind of thing you can do at home all by yourself, which is where you'll no doubt be spending a lot of time if you're as perverse as I think you are. But there's nothing wrong with staying at home by yourself. All the best people do it. Sometimes they go to Hawaii and spend a lot of time alone in a hotel room. I was not optimistic that I would ever find Mc-Govern alive.

Part of the reason was in the elapsed-time department. Part of it was the negative vibratory area created by reading the weird little booklet Hoover had given to me earlier that evening at Wong & Wong's. Part of my gloomy outlook in general could also be attributed to the poi rolls I'd had later at the hotel along with a number of what Hoover had me infectiously referring to as penis coladas. It wasn't really very funny until you had a few penis coladas. But I didn't have much choice that night; if I wasn't going to laugh I was going to cry.

It wasn't clear to me exactly what, if anything, the disappearance of the *ka'ai* had to do with the disappearance of Carline Ravel, the reporter friend of Hoover's who'd covered the futile search for the missing relics. What, if anything, her disappearance had to do with McGovern's was also totally open to conjecture. What we had, I reflected, along with the moonlight on the ocean, were two missing people and two missing religious objects, all of whom could possibly be said to be interrelated only by the most tenuous, evanescent, red-and-yellow patterns of the o-o feathers of the mind.

It was one o'clock in the morning and I was drinking Kona coffee and poring over the X-rays of the *ka'ai* taken in 1919 and dooming anyone who even gave them a sideways glance. I don't know if it was the pounding of the sea or the pounding of my heart that kept reverberating in my hotel room. The X-rays were genuinely terrifying.

The black-and-white pictures were footnoted in a sick, scientific fashion, totally ignoring the horror of the photographs. For example: "Figure 7. Front and profile X-rays of *ka'ai* 1 taken in 1919 by Benjamin H. Nouskajian. In this composite, made from three overlapping plates for each view, bones do not align perfectly because of shifts during original X-ray photography. Note teeth, ornaments, and metal fragments at bottom, and long metal object near center. (Bishop Museum Photo by Chris Takata.)"

Benjamin and Chris had already stepped on a rainbow, no doubt, and Carline was missing and even Hoover had a hangnail. I had no great desire to go to Jesus in the footsteps of the photographers of the *ka'ai*. The images were truly horrific, however. Gaping-mouthed skulls at the top of each basket, a hodgepodge of twisted bones in the middle, teeth at the bottom of each container. If these seriously macabre objects wouldn't send you to hell, I thought, I'd hate to see what would. As a charismatic atheist, I couldn't afford to take any chances.

Around two and a half bells, I killed the lights and spent another troubled hour or so tossing and turning like the restless ocean outside my window. Ideas were forming in my whirling brain like incipient waves far out to sea. About the time they crashed on the breakers, I crashed on my king-sized bed. And that night I dreamed a dream almost as strange and twisted as life itself. Indeed, as dreams are sometimes wont to do, the dream made life seem almost pale beside it, like the fondly remembered face of a dead lover or the sprinkling of saltshaker stars in the sky that scientists now believe are merely layer upon layer of tightly compressed gas.

To make a long dream short, my friend Bob Neuwirth and I were both young kids who were following a rabbit to Canton, Ohio, on mechanized pogo sticks to see Hank Williams on New Year's Day 1953. Hank conked somewhere along the parade route just as a kindly dentist was telling him how important it was to take good care of his teeth. Instead of seeing Hank, we only got to hear Red Foley and his band singing "Peace in the Valley" from behind a curtain.

"What's the name of the curtain?" I asked Neuwirth.

"It's called the final curtain," he said.

"What's the name of the valley?" I asked.

"It's called the Valley of the Shadow of Death," said Neuwirth.

"What happened to the rabbit?" I asked. I was apparently a highly inquisitive youngster.

"He's riding in the back of a big Cadillac," said Neuwirth. "Say hello to my friend Robert Zimmerman."

Zimmerman was a skinny, restless kid who looked like an adolescent Jesus. One eye was laughing and one was crying.

"Follow that rabbit," he said rather cryptically, "and you'll find your dream."

"But this *is* a dream," I said.

"This ain't a dream," he said. "It ain't life either. It's just a song Hank Williams never got around to writing."

The dream began to degenerate somewhat at this point, yet still it struggled to control my torpid, slumbering subconscious mind, which many contend is the only kind of mind that I have. The dream seemed to move very much like a soap opera. Fragmented images were now popping up like bagels in the ruthlessly happy suburban toaster of a Jewish dentist who never was quite able to achieve the happiness inherent in his toaster. All of life hangs by such a ridiculously fragile thread that I found it mildly ironic when the good-natured fellow began telling me how important it was to take good care of my teeth. There was a 5 percent chance, he said, that I may someday need a crown for my upper baboon's asshole molar but it might be fine forever. Then he smiled and revealed two huge, hideously yellow rabbit teeth in the front of his mouth. He killed himself before my next appointment, leaving me struggling with the decision of whether or not someday to get a crown for my upper baboon's asshole molar. I was beginning to feel confused as to whether this was all a dream or just a song Bob Dylan never got around to writing. I finally realized that the kindly Jewish dentist with the rabbit teeth was God and the crown of which he spoke was intended for me. I was, of course, mildly flattered, but upon reflection I did seem like a reasonable choice for the Messiah. I was skinny. I was Jewish. I was a troublemaker. And my teeth were good.

Dorothy, Alice, Beatrix Potter, Grace Slick, and just about everybody else down through history have followed, chased, killed, eaten, written about, or fucked like rabbits extensively, not to mention what all of these people have managed to do to their dreams. My current dream, unfortunately, was still plodding along, now focusing on the phrase "peace in the valley," with whispered voices coming to me almost unintelligibly along a windy beach. I suddenly saw myself in achingly vivid Technicolor killing a rabbit with a rock, something I once actually had to do in 1966 in a survival training program. I didn't know where the hell I was or why I felt compelled to commit this crime so foreign to my nature. I'd never get to be a Buddhist now. What would Richard Gere think? I was crying. The rabbit was whimpering. The wind was whispering peace in the valley, peace in the valley, and at last the words came to me more clearly. "Peace *Corps*," shrieked the wind. "*Waipi'o* Valley." Then I heard McGovern's fabled tape cassette playing softly somewhere down the beach.

Suddenly, a huge, pounding tidal wave was sweeping me away. I woke up and found myself drenched with sweat, sitting up in bed, studying the clock, which read 4:44. The pounding continued, louder than the ocean now. I stumbled over to the door.

"Who's there?" I said.

"Open the fucking door!" shouted a familiar, Brooklyn-accented voice. "Hell, it was easier getting you to throw down that stupid puppet head!"

I opened the door and there stood Rambam, fresh from his adventures on the other side of the world. He wore jeans, sandals, a bright aloha shirt, and an eager, impatient, let-me-at-the-bastards smile.

"Well," he said, "have you found McGovern yet?"

Chapter Thirty

"Let me get this straight," said Rambam, as we watched dawn come up over two mahimahi omelettes with Maui onions, Japanese seaweed, and several other items I didn't recognize. "Because of a dream you had last night and several rather unusual coincidences, you're now telling me you believe McGovern's not on Oahu at all but on the Big Island?"

"Big man," I said. "Big Island."

"That makes about as much sense as everything else you've told me. You'd think with McGovern's life at stake you might try to take a more rational approach to the investigation."

"We've tried the rational approach. We've scoured morgues and mental hospitals and hotels and beaches—"

"Maybe you ought to check the mental hospitals again. After all, it *is* McGovern."

"The world's a fucking mental hospital, Rambam. Somewhere in its convoluted corridors McGovern is either being held against his will or else he's already worm bait. He's been missing for eleven days now."

"If this is some sick prank of his, I'm going to put him in a real hospital."

"It's no prank," I said. "I've told you everything we've been through. The Man-In-Trouble-Lono-Is-Home phone call to my loft in New York. The MIT!—MIT!—MIT! part was definitely McGovern's own voice so he was alive after he disappeared that night from the beach. The bogus kidnapping took about ten years off of my life—"

"A bogus ransom attempt is worse than the real thing because when it's over you're right back where you started. And, it seems, at least to my highly trained professional eye, that's exactly where you are now. Right back where you started."

"Not quite, Sam Spade."

"Let's keep race out of it."

"Let's keep rational approaches out of it. This is Hawaii. You know what they say in Hawaii."

"'Please Do Not Feed the Birds. *Mahalo*'?" said Rambam, reading the little sign on the lanai.

"That's for the haoles. What the old kahunas say is something I've taken somewhat to heart as regards this case. 'The unaimed arrow never misses.'"

"That's the stupidest thing I've ever heard in my life."

"Tell that to an old kahuna when you see him. He'll probably turn you into a jewfish."

"After he takes my wallet. What're you trying to do? Go native to solve a missing persons case?"

"I believe the solution to McGovern's disappearance is deeply intertwined with ancient Hawaiian lore, particularly the missing sacred relics I told you about, the *ka'ai*."

"If you've got something in your *ka'ai* I'll help you get it out."

"The reporter gal, Hoover's friend, has been tracking these stolen relics for over five years. Now she's missing, having just called me the day before from the Big Island proposing to meet at the Bishop Museum where Hoover and I find no sign of her but a bust of the high chief Lono that's the spitting image of McGovern—"

"I think the whole thing's a bust—"

"—and if all that doesn't suggest something, I don't know what does."

"It suggests to me that you've gotten too much sun carrying your friend Stephanie's beach chair."

How Rambam knew about Stephanie's beach chair was a minor mystery in itself, but for the moment, I let it pass. We both had bigger fish to fry and we knew it.

"Forget the *ka'ai*," said Rambam. "What about the FBI? What have they discovered?"

"McCall has good lines of communication with them and with the cops. The answer is that they've both come up with zippo. I'm telling you this case calls for a highly unconventional approach. The two coconut fiber caskets containing the bones of Lono and Liloa are said to have come from the mausoleum of Hale o Keawe at Honaunu or Hale o Liloa in Waipi'o Valley. In 1858 they were removed and placed in the Royal Tomb in Honolulu. From there they went to the Royal Mausoleum and then in 1918 they were sent to the Bishop Museum. There's been no sign of the missing *ka'ai* since they were liberated from the museum, but rumors are rife that they've been reinterred somewhere on the Big Island."

"Pick an island," said Rambam. "Any island."

"I dream of that island. Of that valley. I've been there before, in 1966, when I trained for the Peace Corps in Hilo. My memories of Waipi'o Valley are of a beautiful, pristine, virtually uninhabited place with green hills and waterfalls and sun-blinded beaches. I think the *ka'ai* are somewhere in that valley. I also think that if we can find the *ka'ai*, we'll find McGovern."

"You get the canoe," said Rambam, shaking his head in an incredulous manner, "and I'll help you paddle."

"That's good," I said, "because Hoover, McCall, and Stephanie are going with us, not to mention Stephanie's two dogs, Thisbe and Baby Savannah."

"Then we'll need a pretty fucking big canoe," said Rambam, looking at my forehead rather strangely. "Are you sure you're all right?"

"Of course, I'm all right. We're going to need all the help we can get to find—"

"You've got to be out of your fucking mind to bring all those people over there. For one thing, they're amateurs. For another, you're an amateur. Times have changed since you were there in the sixties. What used to be uninhabited areas are now free zones for international gutter rats, radical independence militias, deranged Vietnam vets, and paranoid marijuana growers with snipers and booby-trapped fields. How would your friend Stephanie like to find one of her cute little dogs at the end of a punji stick?"

"She'd rather find my balls at the end of a bungee cord."

"Then don't take her. She's just going to be trouble. Leave the others behind as well."

"We're all going. I'll have McCall charter a chopper for tomorrow morning."

"You're so damn sure McGovern's over there, why not leave today?"

"Because there's something I've got to do tonight and I can't tell you what it is because you'll think I'm crazy."

"I already think you're crazy," said Rambam. "But if, as you say, the world's a mental hospital, you might just be the perfect ringmaster for this little traveling circus."

"If you feel that way," I said, "you're welcome to stay behind."

"What!" said Rambam. "And give up show business?!"

Chapter Thirty-one

There has to be a sour apple in every barrel and apparently Rambam was it. Hoover, Stephanie, and McCall, all of whom I checked with later that morning, appeared more than willing to follow my dreams, directions, and hunches concerning the expedition to the Big Island. Hoover, who'd become increasingly worried about Carline as well as McGovern, was extremely supportive of both the idea and the Kinkster.

"I can always tell when you're on to something, Kinkyhead," he said in glowing tones. "As I told McGovern and Carline before they both rather unfortunately disappeared: 'The Kinkster may well be the world's greatest living amateur detective. He's never taken on a case that he hasn't brought to a successful conclusion. He's the only detective I know with a totally perfect crime-solving record.'"

"I'm also," I added, "the only detective you know."

"I didn't tell them that," said Hoover.

John McCall was equally enthusiastic about the new turn of events. He took out a large wad of whip-out and waved it in the perfumed air of the islands.

"I always wanted to charter a chopper like they used to do on *Magnum P.I.*," he said.

"Maybe the world *is* a mental hospital," said Rambam, watching the whip-out. "Put that money away before you get mugged by an itinerant lawyer."

Stephanie, of course, took a little more convincing. She was not sold on the notion that practical plans should be based on images that came to one in a dream. She was also not particularly eager to travel anywhere with McCall, Hoover, and Rambam.

"Why do we have to take the Three Stooges?" she asked petulantly from the warm comfort of her beach chair that afternoon.

"We need McCall because he's springing for the chopper, not to mention the whole trip. We need Hoover because he's lived here ten years and one hopes has absorbed some understanding of the people and the culture. And we need Rambam to help rescue McGovern or in case we run into some deranged Vietnam vet."

"What a fucking joke," said Stephanie scornfully. "What's Rambam going to do? Lob a pineapple at him?"

"We're all going as one happy family. Everybody has something to contribute."

"Right. McCall contributes the notion he can buy a life with whipout. Rambam contributes a satellite dish on his head. Hoover contributes his horrendous limericks. And your ass contributes some stupid dream."

"Tell that to Moses and Joseph and Patton and Dr. Martin Luther King. Dreams are important agents for changing the world. The Bible and the history books are full of dreams that prophesied the future and became realities. Dreams are valid tools of detection for they help us explore that greatest of all mysteries, the subconscious mind."

"You should've been a fucking shrink," said Stephanie. "You're crazy and self-absorbed enough and you dress shitty enough. You just don't drive the right kind of car."

"Just because I drive a solar-powered Datsun is no reason to think I wouldn't have made a fine shrink. At least if I were a successful shrink I might get laid more."

"The Elephant Man gets laid more."

I set fire to the south end of a cigar and surveyed the sunburned female flesh scattered across the beach like human driftwood. There were several attractive women in the collection but, of course, none of them compared with Stephanie DuPont. No one in the world compared with Stephanie DuPont. That was the problem.

"There are a number of things that suggest to me that McGovern's on the Big Island."

"And?"

"And the dream I had was sort of the icing on the taro cake. The images in the dream seemed incredibly vivid. The characters were familiar to me. And the background music was that tedious tape cassette McGovern plays incessantly."

"And?"

"And the dream just connected with me almost like it was trying to tell me a story. It was like being in my own personal soap opera."

"What was it?" said Stephanie. "*One Ass to Kiss?*"

I puffed placidly on the cigar for a moment and gazed out at the blue sandwich of the sea and the sky.

"We leave in the morning at oh-eight-hundred," I said.

"*If* McGovern's really there, Dickhead—"

"He is."

"Then you *have* to find him, Friedman."

"I'll do everything humanly possible."

"That's an order," she said, and closed her eyes.

Chapter Thirty-two

I spent most of the afternoon concocting a credible cover story and consulting with various sources and contacts regarding the Big Island. It would undoubtedly be easier to operate if no one in Waipi'o suspected the true nature of our mission. My companions, of course, were rife with suggestions for developing our cover story. Most of them sucked bog water rather severely. Some, however, were not without their merits.

Waipi'o Valley, according to Hoover, was still a very sparsely populated locus, but whether word traveled by conch or by mental telepathy, it nonetheless traveled surprisingly rapidly. If you were searching for a large, recently abducted haole and the kidnappers learned of your intentions, it could be fatal for Big Mac. If the locals, many of whom claimed bloodlines directly back to the dead *alii,* discovered you were trying to locate the missing *ka'ai,* there might soon be a search party searching for your search party.

"We could go over as some kind of traveling entertainment group," Hoover had suggested. "How about the Von Friedman Family Singers?"

"That's about the stupidest idea I've ever heard in my life," I'd told him.

It wasn't long, however, before Rambam came up with something even stupider. It almost appeared as if the gravity of the cover story had eluded my companions. Possibly they did not place great credence in my contention that McGovern was indeed on the island of Hawaii. Possibly they'd lost confidence in my powers of detection. I couldn't say I really blamed them. We'd been out here for more than a week now and all I had to show for it was sand in my pockets and a small white band around my right wrist where I'd recently discarded my wristwatch in a rather misguided Zen-like effort to throw away time. The result was that every five minutes I asked everybody what time it was, a habit, I may say, that appeared to irritate them to the extreme.

"How's this?" said Rambam. "We're a medical team hired by a concerned group of *Hasidim* to investigate the outbreak of a new disease called Finkelstein's syndrome?"

"That's good as far as it goes," I'd responded. "But what is Finkelstein's syndrome?"

"Finkelstein's syndrome is a rare form of leprosy in which the foreskin of gentiles suddenly sloughs off. The *Hasidim* believe these Hawaiian goyim may be a long-lost offshoot of the *maranos*, Portuguese secret Jews who became Christians during the Inquisition. They believe the disease may be God's way of helping these people get back to their roots by making the tips of their roots fall off."

"I can see you've put a lot of thought into this," I'd said. "And there is extensive Portuguese influence in Hawaii. I'll take your suggestion under review."

"I'm so happy," said Rambam. "Does this mean I passed the audition to be an assistant little private dick?"

"It means I wish your whole dick would slough off," I'd said.

McCall's proposal that we be a European tabloid photo team shooting a topless feature on Stephanie DuPont was clearly not going to fly with Stephanie, and given the mood she was currently in, I didn't deem it very practical to even mention it to her. Her own suggestion, though not that far from the truth, also proved to be unsuitable.

"I don't think a beautiful, intelligent, gorgeous, tall, statuesque, witty, well-bred woman inexplicably traveling with four middle-aged assholes is very appropriate for the expedition as I now envisage it," I said. "Of course, nothing is firm yet."

"You've got *that* right," she said.

Sometime after four o'clock Hoover dropped off a small collection of maps and newspaper stories on Waipi'o Valley and the Big Island and I began seriously smoking cigars, pouring Kona coffee, and poring over the materials. The population records, though admittedly vague, indicated that as few as forty families still inhabited the valley, most of the populace having been washed away in the great tsunami of 1946. It was, indeed, the ideal sort of locale out of which cutthroats or kidnappers might operate.

For the next few hours I studied maps and news stories, made a series of phone calls, and ate an endless succession of mango slices the old Hawaiian way, dipped in soy sauce, vinegar, black pepper, and salt. Information continued to flock to my brain like the birds outside on the lanai, searching for residual poi roll crumbs. I spoke to my old Peace Corps pal John Mapes, who helped bring the old training days in Hilo back into focus. I spoke to Kiji Hazelwood, who lived on the Kona Coast of Hawaii and had been kind enough on several occasions to send me killer-bee handpicked coffee beans dried by hippies on her own driveway. I was also fortunate enough to catch my peripatetic legend-friend Willie Nelson just before he was leaving Maui for an extended tour.

Mapes spoke of logistics and changes wrought by time and kahunas. Kiji told me of ghostly processions of night marchers, waterfalls, and kahunas. Willie and I talked about hemp, marijuana, music, religion, philosophy, a joke that's not even suitable for this particular dysfunctional family newspaper, and kahunas. By dinnertime I had kahunas coming out of my ears and was squirting out of both ends from my mango marathon, but otherwise I felt prepared for whatever mysteries the Big Island had to offer.

Stephanie dropped by looking like a young Grace Kelly in a slinky emerald-blue-green sarong outfit just as I was attempting to take my third Nixon of the day. She was mildly irritated about having to wait at the door for a while.

"What *took* you so long?" she demanded.

"I was doing squat-thrusts on the lanai," I said.

"That's good," she said, "because you have the general physique of a Jewish oyster."

"That's not true," I said, offering her some mango slices. "My doctor in Kerrville, Texas, recently told me that I had a very nice physique. Now he may be blind or a homosexual, but—"

"You haven't even asked about the chicks."

"Fuck me dead, mate. How could I have forgotten? How *are* the chicks?"

"Thisbe was ordering room service when I left the room. Baby's been racing around the hallway all afternoon, dashing into any room with the door left open. She ran into one room and jumped on a man's back who was lying on his bed. I could hear the man scream all the way out in the hallway."

"What did the man say?"

"I don't know. I don't speak Japanese."

PART SIX

On the Town

Chapter Thirty-three

"A few more of these penis coladas," said Rambam a short while later at the hotel bar, "and we're not going to need a chopper."

Rambam, McCall, Stephanie, and myself were holding down a seaside table waiting for Hoover to finish filing a story for the *Advertiser*. I'd promised to take everybody to dinner and I planned to make it something special. After all, if we were successful in locating McGovern on the Big Island, this could well be our last night together in Honolulu. Even if you're merely hopping to another island, there's always a strangely poignant touch of sadness in every Hawaiian farewell. I don't know if it was our imminent departure, the veil of mystery and danger awaiting us, or the penis coladas, but I was beginning to feel just a sun-bleached hair sentimental.

"While we wait for Hoover," I said, "I'd just like to say that I've come to think of all of you as the Village Irregulars West and I've come to depend upon your services and abilities—"

"Shut *up*, asshole," said Stephanie. "You're drunk."

"Just because we don't always see eye to eye on everything—"

"Of *course* we don't see eye to eye, Friedman," said Stephanie. "I'm taller than all of you."

"Except me," said Rambam.

"Sure," said Stephanie. "If you like to count the satellite dish on your head."

"I'd like to ram the satellite dish down your throat," said Rambam.

"Lucky for you I'm Jewish and we don't believe in violence against women."

"You don't believe in picking up the check either," said McCall, in a rather unfortunate effort at levity.

"People have gotten themselves thrown out of helicopters for remarks like that," said Rambam. "Not to mention bar mitzvah receptions."

"How about another penis colada, Dickhead?" said Stephanie.

"I think our waitress passed away," I said. "But I'll get it for you."

"You're my hero," said Stephanie in a bored and toneless voice.

"Where the hell's Hoover?" said Rambam. "If he disappears we've got ourselves a reporter hat trick."

"He won't disappear," I said. "And we will find McGovern on Hawaii."

"I'd drink to that," said Stephanie dryly. "If I had a fucking drink."

"I'll take care of it. Oh, miss," I said, as the waitress flew by like a seagull.

"What a joke," said Stephanie.

Moments later, not only had another round of drinks arrived for everyone, but so had Hoover. I was pleased to hear him express great confidence in my plan to search for McGovern in Waipi'o Valley. Rambam was clearly somewhat skeptical. "Pick an island," he'd said. "Any island." As far as McCall and Stephanie were concerned, it didn't appear as if they gave much credence to the theory that McGovern and the missing *ka'ai* were interwoven with each other tighter than a sennit basket.

"What Kinkyhead is proposing," said Hoover, "is very logical. The Waipi'o Valley is so sparsely populated and so inaccessible even today that communication with the outside can be almost impossible. If I were going to kidnap Stephanie, for instance, that'd be where I'd keep her. I'd tie her up and gag her and make her listen to me recite limericks."

"I'd kill myself immediately," said Stephanie. "I'd jump in the nearest volcano."

"There are no volcanoes in Waipi'o," said Hoover. "Only rivers and palis, and jungle trails, and, when it rains, lots and lots of waterfalls."

"One of which has already provided a possible clue of singular importance," I said.

"Care to tell us about it, Deerstalker Dick?" said Stephanie.

"All in good time, Twatson."

"Friedman! I'm warning you—"

"And then, of course," continued Hoover obliviously, "there's the night marchers."

"Night marchers?" said McCall warily.

"Ghostly processions of dead *aliis* and their soldiers," said Hoover. "They march with drums and torches. Some people hear 'em. Some people see 'em. Some people hear *and* see 'em. Unfortunately, almost no one who's ever seen 'em has lived to tell about it."

"Looks like a few survivors over there," said Rambam, gesturing discreetly in the direction of a four-piece octogenarian band warming up in the bar.

The band was known as the Makai Strings. In Hawaii there are only two directions: *makai* means toward the sea; *mauka* means toward the mountains. The four players, two men and two women, had the bright-eyed, weathered visage of souls who'd lived at the islands longer than the rest of us had lived everywhere else. The two men wore white shirts with kukui nut leis and played steel and guitar, and the two women wore colorful old-fashioned dresses with floral leis and played ukeleles. They played a short set of native Hawaiian folk music mixed with popular island tunes. They seemed friendly, fragile, joyful, and sad, like the history of Hawaii itself, with the women sometimes shy, sometimes seeming to almost flirt with the audience. They played "Beautiful Kauai." They played "Blue Hawaii." The lilting steel guitar, the ukeleles, the frail voices, the old eyes shining like sunlight on water, all combined to create a nimble portrayal of a magical culture that was fading faster than words and music could convey.

The songs rolled like gentle waves of sound over the sun-burnished shoulders of the patrons of the bar. Some seemed oblivious to the music; some seemed mesmerized by it. But the Hawaii of the Makai Strings was already gone. The missionaries, the Americans, the Japanese, the sugar barons, the pineapple kings, leprosy, measles, smallpox, influenza, and that most cruel and relentless disease of them all—time—had either decimated or assimilated the children of the rainbow, and only God knows which fate is worse. The beauty of old Hawaii lived again, however, if only in the raw, dreamy eyes of four ancient haoles who must've been handsome, feisty people once, and now played stoically—no, cheerfully—in the hotel bar, with gray heads full of memories and each with both hands on the strings and one foot in the grave.

The Makai Strings' first set ended fittingly with "Aloha Oe," the song written in prison by Queen Liliukalani for her dead husband, King Kalakaua. "My love be with you till we meet again." But some of us never do. I thought of Robert Louis Stevenson telling stories under the banyan tree to Ka'iulani, the teenage princess of Hawaii, the last princess of Hawaii, the princess who would never be queen because her kingdom was lost like a sand castle, the princess who died younger than Hank Williams but older than John Keats, the princess who was loved by her people and for whom the royal peacocks cried at the precise moment of her death, whose lovely, fetching portrait now stares through the tourists at the Royal Hawaiian Hotel with eyes full of mischief and tragedy, timeless as the tropical rain.

I thought of the prophetic poem Stevenson had written for Ka'iulani and inscribed in her little red autograph book before she left for schooling in Great Britain. The banyan tree, rather predictably, was cut down in the name of urban development, but a cutting was saved and replanted and now flourishes in the playground of the Princess Ka'iulani Elementary School in Honolulu. Beneath the tree the poem is engraved upon a brass plaque. So, in a real sense, in the way of this world, the poem and the tree still stand. The verse is recorded as follows:

> Forth from her land to mine she goes,
> The island maid, the island rose,
> Light of heart and bright of face:
> The daughter of a double race.
> Her islands here, in Southern sun,
> Shall mourn their Ka'iulani gone,
> And I, in her dear banyan shade,
> Look vainly for my little maid.

"A fond embrace," the band was singing, "until we meet again." Then "Aloha Oe" was over and I noticed a tear in Stephanie's eye. For all I know there may have been one in my own as well. Could've been the soft tug of history and time and the moments that transcend them both. For everything good and great and beautiful always happens in a moment. That's why they last forever.

A short while later, as I signaled to the waitress to drop the hatchet, I observed that Hoover was still running on about the night marchers. He did seem to have an almost clinical recall on certain arcane subjects, the *ka'ai* and the night marchers being two of them.

"—and your only hope of survival if you see them," Hoover was saying, "is if you happen to be a direct blood descendant of the *alii*. Even then you're probably dead meat. If you're not a direct descendant there's only one long shot for you—and I'm not making this up— it's an ancient *kapu,* a forbidden thing to see. What you have to do, if you happen to be unfortunate enough to see the night marchers, is strip off all your clothes and, stark naked, lie prostrate on the ground, flat on your stomach."

"Here's to Stephanie seeing the night marchers," I said.

"Here's to Friedman *not* seeing them," she said.

Chapter Thirty-four

"When you said you were taking us all out for dinner," said McCall an hour later, "I didn't realize you meant the Don Ho Show."

"They serve dinner," I said, as I gestured around us to the elderly sets of tourists in matching haole shirts being served identical rubber chicken platters by a vast team of waiters.

"You've got to hand it to Kinky," said Rambam. "He's got class."

"What's wrong with having dinner at the Don Ho Show?" I said. "The demographics are terrific."

"You're right, Dickhead," said Stephanie. "It's the only place in town you guys could go where you'd be the youngest, hippest people in the crowd."

"I don't know about hippest," said Hoover. "That guy with the bicycle horn on his aluminum walker looks pretty cool."

"Let me tell you the real reason we're here," I said, with some little irritation. "Lest we forget, we're trying to find McGovern."

"He's too young to be in this audience," said McCall.

"Look," I said, as the waiter placed some kind of pineapple chicken dish in front of me, "I've seen this show about four times. My pants were caught in the seat. I tried to signal the usher—"

"Why didn't you strip out of your pants," said Stephanie, "and lie prostrate on the floor stark naked while Don Ho was performing?"

"Because at least one of those times," I said, "I was performing with him. He was kind enough to invite me up on stage with him and I sang 'Get Your Biscuits in the Oven and Your Buns in the Bed' and 'Ol' Ben Lucas (Had a Lotta Mucus)'."

"That's biting the hand that feeds you," said Hoover.

"What are you talking about?" I ejaculated. "The crowd loved it!"

"Have you looked at this crowd lately?" said Rambam. "Half of them are in the grip of a fairly tertiary stage of senility."

"And the other half are already dead," said Hoover.

"And they're only talking about *our* table," said Stephanie.

"The point is," I said, "that I know Don Ho. We're friends. He can help us. Not only was he entertaining the troops during the French and Indian War—"

"Entertaining the Indians most likely," said Hoover.

"Knowing Don's sympathies," I said, "you're probably right. But he's entertained people around the world since we were jumping rope in the school yard and—and this is important—he knows as much about Hawaiian history, culture, myth, and legend as many kahunas. In fact, I might say Don Ho is my kahuna."

"Why don't you start a new religious sect," said Rambam.

"Don't you see," I said, lowering my voice to a whisper. "In a huge, almost uninhabited gorge like Waipi'o, it may be easier to locate the *ka'ai* than to find McGovern, not to mention a hell of a lot less dangerous. And I'm convinced where we find one, we'll find the other."

"What about Carline?" whispered Hoover.

"We'll find her, too," I whispered. "If she's alive."

"Why would McGovern be alive," Hoover hissed, "and Carline dead?"

"Because Carline wasn't in the dream," I said.

"Why're you idiots whispering?" said Rambam. "These people couldn't hear you if you had a bullhorn."

"What'd he say?" asked McCall.

If you've been to Hawaii and never seen Don Ho, you're a rare individual. You've also missed something unique and special. If you come in expecting the show to be slick and commercial and tourist-pleasing, you won't be wrong. But at some indefinable point in the evening, possibly the second time Ho performs his megahit "Tiny Bubbles," something that must be termed poignant seems to steal across your heart. Ho and his colorful ensemble in some strange fashion almost appear to epitomize the magic that was and sometimes still is Hawaii. I'm not going to tell you more for fear of demystifying the experience for you. But there is a self-deprecating sense of humor and a sense of grace about Don Ho that puts him up there in my timeless Hawaiian trinity along with, of course, Damien and the Duke.

"So we're going to meet him in his dressing room?" asked Rambam after the show.

"That's right," I said, with a faint touch of pride. "Stick with the Kinkster and I could probably get you in to see the Pope."

"I'd rather see Don Ho," said Rambam.

"Ladies and gentlemen," said an announcer's voice over the PA system. "Mr. Ho has graciously agreed to have his photograph taken with anyone in the audience wishing to come by his dressing room. He will also autograph tapes, cassettes, and T-shirts, which are available in the lobby. *Mahalo* and aloha."

"Get in line, Dickhead," said Stephanie.

We waited the approximate length of the French and Indian War, but we finally got in to see Ho. He was friendly and charming and seemed to have fond memories of meeting me before. He also seemed to have fond memories of meeting Stephanie before, which, of course, he hadn't. He did not quite have Willie Nelson's Zen-Texan ability to make you think you were the only person in the world when you were talking with him. He did, however, have the natural ability to make you feel at home, which, of course, you weren't, and to make you feel like somebody important, which no doubt you were if indeed God is watching every Edith Piaf.

After we'd all exchanged phone numbers and hobbies for a while, I signaled the Irregulars West to please leave the building, which, after a few autographs and alohas and a kiss for Mr. Ho from Stephanie, they eventually, if rather grudgingly, did. If you plan to tell a Hawaiian you're searching for the missing *ka'ai*, it always goes down better without witnesses.

After we'd closed the dressing room door, I told Ho about McGovern, the Lono connection, and the possible involvement of the *ka'ai*, which I now strongly suspected in the disappearance of McGovern and Carline Ravel. First, he shook his head and muttered a few choice words in Hawaiian. Then he spoke to me for about five or ten minutes in the fatherly tones of a teacher, a rabbi, or a kahuna. Clearly, he understood my determination, anxiety, and frustration where McGovern was concerned. He also felt "like all true Hawaiians" that the *ka'ai* should not be disturbed again. He thought that searching for them was morally wrong and possibly extremely dangerous as well. With my friend McGovern in mind, he then provided me with some valuable spiritual tips that I'd not found in any of Carline's or Hoover's materials. Though he had deep misgivings, he genuinely wished me success on my endeavor, almost in the conflicted manner of an Irish father whose son is being sent to fight in the service of the king.

Chapter Thirty-five

It was time for visions and revisions. Walking at midnight down Kalakaua Boulevard through the noisy neon nightlife of Honolulu, past the crashing hymn of the sea, with the dark and sharp outline of Diamond Head in view, each of us appeared to almost be an island unto himself. I could not vouch for what the others were thinking. As for myself, Don Ho's comments, dysjunctified as they were, were flooding my brain like a red tide. We were in sight of the hotel with liftoff less than eight hours away when Stephanie finally made reference to the mortal issues at hand.

"The chicks are very excited about the trip tomorrow morning," she said.

"*What* chicks?" said Rambam incredulously.

"I don't think you'll be interested in these particular chicks," said McCall. "One's a Yorkie and one's a Maltese. Of course, the Maltese is kind of cute."

"Wait a minute," said Rambam. "We're not taking two yapping little lapdogs to Hawaii tomorrow."

"We're *not* leaving them *here*," shrieked Stephanie, instantly on the verge of hysteria.

"You'll get to like Baby Savannah and Thisbe, Rambam," I said encouragingly. "Once they've ice-picked your brain for about eleven hours you'll kind of begin to tune it out."

"You people are amazing," said Rambam in disgust and disbelief.

"We're going into a hostile environment where we may encounter the scumbags who've already made two people disappear and you're bringing along this ball-busting princess and her two pampered, pedigreed pooches? Have you finally lost your mind, Kinky? The mission itself is dangerous. Taking them along is suicide."

"We were counting on you for protection," said Stephanie coyly. "We'd heard that Rambam the Jewish Superman could whip anybody with his nose tied behind his back."

"Remarks like that," said Rambam cooly, "could get little doggies thrown out of helicopters."

"Try it," said Stephanie, with ice in her voice, "and your balls'll be flyin' out right after them."

"I hate to change the subject," said Hoover with a mischievous grin, "but since we're all leaving in the morning for Hawaii, it might be instructive to hear what Don Ho had to say to Kinkyhead here."

"He said: 'Ti—ny bubbles . . . iiinnn the wine,'" sang McCall, who was already borderline monstered himself.

"C'mon, Kinkyhead!" persevered Hoover. "We're going into uncharted territory here. Tell us what he told you."

"Well, after I ran down what my plan was," I said, "Ho just shook his head a while and muttered a few words in Hawaiian."

"What were they?" asked Stephanie eagerly. "I've got my *Instant Hawaiian Guide to Key Words and Colorful Phrases* right here in my purse."

"The first word he said was *pupule!*"

Stephanie thumbed through the little book under a street lamp with remarkable dexterity. In almost no time she'd found the translation.

"It means 'crazy!'" she said. "What was the second word?"

"The second word was *hupo!*" I said.

I calmly set fire to a fresh cigar as Stephanie riffled through the little book again. This was getting rather tedious, not to say mildly embarrassing.

"I've *got* it," shouted Stephanie proudly. "It means 'fool!' Friedman. It means *fool!*"

"I heard you the first time," I said. "I may be a fool but I'm not an idiot."

"What else did he say?" shrieked Stephanie, as if she'd drawn blood. "Come *on*, Dickhead! It could be *important!*"

"All right," I said, as offhandedly as possible, considering that everyone had gathered around me to hear Don Ho's precious utterances. "It's quite understandable that Ho thought the mission to be highly risky. Also, he's opposed to anybody disturbing the sacred *ka'ai*. Nevertheless, he was very supportive—"

"*Dick*head," said Stephanie. "What other Hawaiian words did he *say?*"

"He said: '*Awiwi! Pololi au!*'"

"Let's see," said Stephanie, Quickly thumbing through her little book. "That's a hard one to find."

"Probably just some words of encouragement for the trip," I suggested.

"That's wishful thinking," said Stephanie. "Here it is. '*Awiwi! Pololi au!*'"

"So what the hell does it mean?" I said impatiently.

"I'll tell you what it means, Friedman," said Stephanie with very little effort at concealing her glee. "It means: 'Be quick! I'm hungry!'"

"Let's not judge Don Ho's contribution by a few roughly translated phrases he might've uttered in haste after a long, strenuous performance. During the course of our conversation he did discuss some very pertinent things with me."

"Such as?" said Rambam.

"He himself puts much stock in dreams. Many Hawaiians dream of night marchers. Ho admitted he dreams of them himself."

"And?" said Stephanie.

"And they march through his dreams, carrying torches, beating drums, and playing nose flutes."

"And gay Hawaiians," said Rambam, "dream of night marchers playing skin flutes."

"There's more," I said, ignoring the taunts of the crowd. "Ho claims there are many eyewitnesses to the night marchers alive today but all of them observed the awesome spectacle as children. Ho suspects the deadly *alii* spare children because they're innocent and brave.

"Now in the burial chant of Kamehameha," I continued, "at least, according to Ho, there is a mention of Hokuahiahi, the Hawaiian word for the planet Venus and a reference to looking out to sea at the point where Venus rises. Waipi'o, you understand, has only a narrow channel to the ocean and this is by one of its two major waterfalls. I'm not sure which one, but I plan to find out."

"Why is this so important?" asked Rambam, in a tone of genuine interest.

"Because in ancient times Kamehameha lived here, the king who united the entire island chain—"

"Except Kauai—" said Stephanie.

"All my little helpful history scholars," I said. "But she's right, though the point is rather irrelevant. In the thirteenth or fourteenth century using cannons for the first time, which the Hawaiians called 'red-mouthed guns,' he conquered the other islands. Waipi'o had over fifty thousand inhabitants and all the sacred bones and treasures of the dead *alii* were buried there. My friend Kiji Hazelwood, who lives on the Big Island, told me an interesting story recently. It was about a friend of hers who was standing in a waterfall at Waipi'o two years ago. He reached down and found a strange wooden object on the floor of the waterfall—"

"It was Friedman's dick," said Stephanie, but this time no one laughed. For once I seemed to have the crowd with me. Even Stephanie.

"What was it?" asked Hoover.

"It was an ancient wooden statue, Watson. Now if you put that anecdote together with Don Ho's tidbit about standing at the only point in Waipi'o facing east where you can see Venus rising from the sea by a waterfall, you've found the mystical burial place of the ancient Hawaiian kingdom. You've also found the place where the missing *ka'ai* have almost certainly been reburied. And if you find that place, whether by means of a dream or a chain of deductive reasoning, or a little bit of both, I believe you'll find McGovern and Carline."

"Now you're talkin', Kinkyhead," said Hoover.

"It makes sense," said McCall.

"I'll bring scuba gear for the waterfall," said Stephanie.

"I'll bring some protection," said Rambam.

"Bullets won't work against night marchers," said Hoover.

"Don't tell me you really believe in the night marchers?" said Rambam.

"White doctors call it heart failure," said Hoover, "but Hawaiians see it differently. What else can you conclude when every few months or so beside some thousand-year-old forest trail you find a dead guy lying prostrate on the ground stark naked?"

"Maybe they were trying to jump the bones of a very agile hula dancer," said Rambam.

In the hotel bar a few moments later, we all had a farewell-to-Honolulu penis colada. The mood had turned more upbeat and determined, or maybe it was merely more fatalistic. We watched the palm trees swaying in the sultry night air, the lights of the city twinkling in the distance, and the moonlight reflecting on the ocean in great, luminous ropes of infinity that rigged and held these dark sparkling island-jewels of the sea together in a manner in which even Kamehameha the Great could only dream. And as my thoughts turned to mortality and eternity, inevitably, I thought of McGovern.

"There's a very real chance," I said, "that he's still alive. There's no electricity, no lights, no phones in Waipi'o Valley."

"No pool,"said McCall. "No pets."

"That means you," said Rambam, pointing his finger at Stephanie.

"*Elemakuli ule*," said Stephanie.

"Which means?" said Rambam.

"Elderly man's penis," said Stephanie.

"If they've somehow connected McGovern with Lono," I said, "he might well be receiving the full royal treatment. But time is running out. The last thing Don Ho said to me was: 'Remember, they thought Captain Cook was a god once, too.'"

PART SEVEN

On the Move

Chapter Thirty-six

What should've been a short chopper hop to Hilo turned out to be an interminable nightmare with Rambam crabbing at Stephanie, Stephanie crabbing at me, and Thisbe and Baby Savannah developing a seemingly quite inexplicable fondness for Rambam that, in turn, prolonged and exacerbated his crabbing at Stephanie, which caused her, as women will invariably do, to quite illogically take it out on me. Hoover, at one point, attempted to leaven the situation with a contemporaneous, if rather crude, limerick that did not fly particularly well. Thisbe and Baby Savannah did not fly particularly well either, spending most of their time harassing Rambam, ice-picking everyone's brains out, shitting and pissing in excitement or vindictiveness for being made to ride in the chopper, and in Thisbe's case, having recently consumed a large Hawaiian breakfast at the hotel, vomiting profusely into John McCall's lap, causing him to become quite nauseous himself and overinject himself with insulin thereby propelling him into what appeared to be a diabetic coma, which, I suppose, was as good a way as any to survive the experience.

It must be noted that the view, if anyone had the time or the temperament to observe it, was breathtaking. The Big Island in the morning sunlight sparkled like a tennis bracelet of the gods. The ocean that caressed its curving shoreline was a thing of purity and depth and beauty, qualities that seemed to be so often lacking in those who gazed down upon it. And there was something more: a wildness, a restlessness, a febrile excitement that even beautiful Oahu could not match.

As McCall had arranged, we were met at the heliport near Hilo by our guide and driver, Kekoa, which, he explained, means "the courageous one." He would need all the courageousness he could muster, I figured, to handle our little entourage. We got into the four-wheeled Land Rover without mishap and headed for that violent, green gouge in the earth that I now remembered as little more than a long-ago blur. It'd been thirty-three years since my only trip to Waipi'o Valley and all I remembered distinctly was killing a rabbit to demonstrate to some forgotten Peace Corps instructor that I could survive in the wilderness. I hadn't wanted to kill the rabbit. I'd wanted to kill the Peace Corps instructor. He'd caused the death of a harmless rabbit for no reason whatsoever. Killing a rabbit, unless you're really starving to death, has never brought anyone closer to God. It's never even stopped anyone from killing himself. But this time, thank Christ, I wasn't here to kill a rabbit. I was here to save a man.

The ride out to Waipi'o awakened vague memory fragments in my brain. Cold showers. Warm waterfalls. Green taro patches that looked like a drunken chessboard. Paul and Kay Matsumoto's friendly little general store where John Mapes and I used to hang out when we got tired of learning how to save the world. Drinking Primo Beer in ancient, horseshoe-shaped bars open to the street with giant military cargo planes circling continuously with a loud, dull, somnolent roar. Maybe they were flying supplies for Vietnam. Maybe these planes were just built to circle horseshoe-shaped bars. I also remembered the first time I met John Mapes. He was the first white man I ever saw wearing a sarong. The fact that he subsequently became one of my closest friends in Peace Corps training does not necessarily indicate latent homosexuality on my part. All of this, of course, was long before I met Mike McGovern, a man whose enormous consumption of alcohol and enormous capacity for living life helped lead me down the not unpleasant path to depravity, along which I made a lot of new memories that jostled the old memories out of my head and eventually resulted in my waking up one day and realizing I'd forgotten the first half of my life.

"Have you been to Hawaii before?" Kekoa was asking.

"I was in Hilo in sixty-six," I said. "With the Peace Corps."

"I wasn't born then," said the guide.

"Neither was anybody else," said Stephanie. She, Rambam, and Kekoa all laughed. McCall, Hoover, and I smiled ruefully. Baby Savannah and Thisbe ice-picked everybody's brains.

"So you're on vacation?" asked the courageously persistent Kekoa.

"No," said Hoover. "We're a friendly group of traveling homosexuals. We're acrobats actually. We're sort of a gay circus."

"Are the dogs part of the act?" asked Kekoa.

"No," said Rambam. "They're our agents."

"Who's the wahine?" asked Kekoa.

"I'm their manager," said Stephanie imperiously.

Kekoa wasn't buying our story, but it was better than his finding out the truth. Before long we'd reached a lookout site over Waipi'o Valley. Not until I shoveled a glance into the green abyss did I realize what we were truly up against. The taro patches were still there all right. The crazy drunken giants were playing chess again. But how would we find that other drunken giant? This was not the little green valley I grew up in in Texas. This gouge in the earth was colossal. The palis seemed to drop dizzyingly straight down forever.

"The valley," said Kekoa, "is a mile wide and six miles deep. That zigzag trail you see is a thousand years old. It's probably safer than the road, though. Lots of malihinis try to drive their own cars down it. That's okay. But coming back up is very steep. They hit the brakes and then they stall. The next thing you know away they go. We lose more malihinis that way."

"What're malihinis?" asked McCall.

"They're homosexuals," said Stephanie, clutching the two little dogs close to the dizzying palis of her breasts.

Kekoa laughed his friendly Hawaiian laugh again. He looked quizzically at Stephanie. She gave him a stunner of a smile and she winked at him. At that moment I'm sure he felt like the luckiest guide in the world.

"Malihinis are newcomers," he said. "Into this valley we all go as newcomers."

We learned some history from Kekoa on the way down, which was a good thing because it provided some diversion from a trip that was definitely not for the fainthearted. Kamehameha had grown up in this valley from the time he was three months old until he was fifteen. Four *heiaus*, or ancient temples, were still in the valley, some of them dating from A.D. 680. One of them was the site where a certain chief Umi habitually sacrificed eighty human victims at a time.

According to Kekoa, Waipi'o was the doorway to Lua O Milu, the Hawaiian legendary version of hell. Processions of ghosts return to the underworld every year at a mysterious point along the shore. Night marchers are heard but not often seen throughout the area. Kekoa himself, if he was to be believed, had once seen a long line of torches heading up the old zigzag path. He could hear a thousand voices chanting.

"Did you strip off your clothes and throw yourself prostrate upon the ground stark naked?" asked Hoover.

"Are you *sure* you guys aren't homosexuals?" asked Kekoa.

A while later, Kekoa pointed out in the distance the tallest waterfall in Hawaii. I looked and listened with heightened interest. We were closing in.

"The name of the waterfall is Hiilawe," said Kekoa. "According to legend Hiilawe was a princess who fell in love with Kakalaoa. They wanted to get married but their families wouldn't allow it. She cried and cried until the waterfall was created and Kakalaoa changed himself into the big rock that is now at the bottom of the cascade of water. He did this so Hiilawe's tears might fall upon him."

"It's kind of like the legend of Kinkyhead and Stephanie," said Hoover.

"There's only one difference," said Stephanie. "Instead of crying I'd be vomiting at the thought of marrying Friedman."

Maybe it was one of those cosmic coincidences that occasionally occur in life. Maybe it was the torturously steep drive. Maybe it was the words themselves. Whatever the reason, Thisbe promptly vomited again into John McCall's lap.

Chapter Thirty-seven

By late in the afternoon we were safely ensconced in a forlorn little inn that boasted virtually no sign of human habitation. That was fine with me. People have been fucking up this world since the unicorn disappeared and they'd no doubt keep it up until Jesus came back in a Thunderbird. As we'd said our alohas to our guide Kekoa, Rambam had confided to him the nature of our true mission.

"We're a medical team," he'd told him so pathologically convincingly that I practically believed him myself. "We're doing some field research on a rare disease called Finkelstein's syndrome."

Kekoa had shaken hands a little uncertainly with Rambam, then hopped back into the Land Rover. "I think I've heard of that," he'd said.

After watching Kekoa's happy Hawaiian head disappear up the road at about a ninety-nine-degree angle, four men, one woman, and two little dogs settled into our new accommodations. The only sign of humanity was an octogenarian Japanese who, in an earlier incarnation, looked like he might've been a gardener in Beverly Hills, but now, after coping with our clamorous arrival, was quite possibly contemplating hara-kiri in the backyard somewhere.

"What do you mean, 'The toilet is down the hall'?" Stephanie was shrieking.

"Darling, these are primitive conditions," I reasoned. "I know it's not the Ritz Hotel in Paris, but I'd like to see each of us reach inside himself and find the strength to deal with the situation."

"I'd like to see you reach inside yourself and find a personality," she said.

"I do look forward to seeing the two of us share a room together," I said.

"And I look forward to seeing your obituary," said Stephanie dreamily. "We'd show up for your funeral in my black Porsche. The chicks would each have little black ribbons in their hair. I'd be wearing a very fashionable wide black hat with a veil, a *very* short black dress, and *very* tall black stilettoes. And I'd carry a Gucci purse, of course, with your last will and testament inside leaving everything to me and the chicks. Then we'd wheel out of there in the Porsche and people would say, 'Who was that mysterious, gorgeous woman with the two mysterious, gorgeous little dogs?' And someone would say, 'Maybe it was the Aga Khan's daughter.' And somebody else would say, 'Maybe it's Friedman's daughter.' And a third person—"

"That's probably all that'd be there," I said.

"And the third person would say, 'Maybe it's the wrong funeral.'"

"What the hell," I said. "It's probably worth croaking just to see you in that outfit."

"That's *right*," she said. "And if you haven't noticed, Dickhead, it's also worth living for."

"I *have* noticed," I said. "I've also noticed that the toilet's down the hall."

"This is the last time I'm staying in a one-star hotel."

"Speaking of stars," I said, "do you know what Venus looks like?"

"Of course, Fuckbrain. I see her likeness every time I look in a mirror."

"The *star*," I said. "Not the goddess. We've got to see if we can spot Venus from the waterfall tonight."

"If we do," said Stephanie, "I'm going to make a wish."

"What for, darling?"

"Room service," she said.

Chapter Thirty-eight

We didn't get to the Hiilawe waterfall that night. For one thing, objects in the rearview mirror had apparently seemed closer than they were. It was a full day's hike just to get to the place and the rumblings among the crew were that more research in the areas of logistics, astronomy, and how to deal with night marchers might be in order. McCall began organizing food and supplies for the expedition. Rambam struck up a lengthy, if rather one-sided, conversation with the octogenarian Japanese landlord. And Hoover set out across the wilderness to chat up the only other human being in the vicinity, a neighboring taro farmer who was so far away from us that, to the naked eye, he resembled little more than an ant wearing a minuscule straw hat.

While my concern for McGovern was mounting, it was probably a good thing that we took a bit more time to plot out the best route to reach the waterfall. Upon Hoover's return from his little pidgin tête-à-tête with the taro farmer, we realized the trip was not one to be embarked upon lightly. Indeed, within the old man's memory, over the years several parties that embarked upon the trip had never embarked upon anything else again, having somewhat erroneously followed the ancient zigzag trail to hell instead.

Hoover, it quickly became apparent, had taken copious notes on how to avoid the pitfalls of the previous parties. However, in typical Hooverian fashion, and quite maddeningly to me, he refused to divulge what he'd learned until he had a chance "to review the mater-

175

ial." I reminded him that lives were at stake if we didn't reach the fucking waterfall yesterday.

"I'll remind you, Kinkyhead," said Hoover in world-weary, patronizing tones, "that if we don't reach that fucking waterfall, we'll wander around lost forever because there's no place else in the foreseeable vicinity to reach. The taro farmer has already expressed a strong disinclination to be a one-man search party. He advises us specifically not to attempt this trek to the waterfall. He says it's much harder than it looks—"

"It looks pretty goddamn hard," said Rambam.

"That's the point," said Hoover. "He doesn't think we can do it. He thinks we'll blither around lost until things devolve into a *Lord of the Flies* situation—"

"He didn't say that," said Rambam.

"Not in so many words," said Hoover. "But that's what he meant. Pidgin is so simple that it's pretty difficult to misunderstand."

"What else did he say," I asked, "that you feel at liberty to tell us?"

"He said if we get lost out there, the *Lord of the Flies* situation could quickly degenerate into cannibalism—"

"What a joke," said Stephanie scornfully.

"He said," continued Hoover, "that circumstances could conceivably arise in which the members of the Friedman party, for our very survival, might have to eat Stephanie."

"Sounds like a plan," I said.

"Rambam would probably just love to volunteer to shoot my ass," said Stephanie.

"Who said anything about shooting your ass?" said Rambam. "Kinky's just hoping he gets the opportunity to eat you."

"Sounds like a plan," I said.

"Before that happens," said Stephanie, "Friedman may get the opportunity to see me cut off his balls and sprinkle them on top of a macadamia nut tart. It's a mouthwatering tropical dessert. Serves five."

"You can share that recipe with McGovern," I said, "if he's still alive when we find him. We leave for the waterfall at dawn. That is, if everyone still wants to go."

Life turns on a dime, they say. In like manner, the mood changed drastically from nervous banter to an almost Alamo ambience, fraught with shades of mortality, lines in the sand, and moonlight on the water that we could not see. From the primeval darkness of the valley spun the spirits of death and doubt and duty and in the hopelessly faraway vaudeville sky flapped the feathered star-crossed wings of now and never and forever.

"And now the moment of reckoning is upon us," I said to the little group of companions huddled around me. "His Kinkyship sails at dawn! Those who choose to follow me—"

"Shut *up*, asshole," said Stephanie. "Everybody's *going*. Do you think we all came this far just to share the toilet down the hall?"

"And it's been especially nice," said Rambam, "with Kinky squirtin' out of both ends."

"Don't remind me," said Stephanie, walking away. "I've got to feed the chicks."

"I hope you plan to leave them behind tomorrow," said Rambam.

"I'd *like* to leave *you* behind tomorrow," said Stephanie, not bothering to look back.

"You're signing the death warrants on those two little dogs if you let her bring them," said Rambam, after Stephanie had disappeared into the sad little hotel.

"He's right," said Hoover. "The taro farmer said the terrain is full of palis and pools and fissures and lava tubes. If those dogs get lost, they'll be hors d'oeuves for one of the ninety-seven million wild pigs that roam around here at night."

"With Kinky's nuts sprinkled on top," said McCall, looking up momentarily from his supply lists.

"We have no choice, gentlemen," I said. "If we make it to the waterfall and discover that it affords the view to the sea, we will be very close to discovering what has become of McGovern and Carline Ravel. It's also my belief that we will be standing nearer than any modern men to the secret burial caves of the ancient Hawaiians."

"The taro farmer," said Hoover, "says there's nothing special about that waterfall."

"Fuck the taro farmer," I said.

That night I slept fitfully. Maybe I was just keyed up about the hike the next morning to the waterfall. Maybe it was the bugs and mosquitoes that kept coming to the Coleman lanterns. Maybe it was the stress of knowing how far we'd come and how close I believed us to be. Or maybe it was the strangely recurring auditory hallucinations I appeared to be experiencing of muffled drums in the distance of a dream.

PART EIGHT

On the Trail

Chapter Thirty-nine

By late morning I didn't care whether the zigzag trail led to hell or not, because for all practical purposes we were already there. We'd been up and down several terrifyingly steep palis and from our current position, a small dry riverbed between Mount Everest and Mount Sinai, the waterfall was no longer in sight. The day was hotter than a blast furnace and all five of us were panting like perverts and sweating like boar-hogs, several of which we'd had a close encounter with earlier in the morning.

It wasn't the cigar smoking that was fagging me as much as the fact that Stephanie and I were each equipped with Louis Vuitton pet carriers and Thisbe, whom I was carrying, weighed considerably more than Baby Savannah. After five hours of hiking I wasn't even sure that Thisbe was a Yorkie.

"Maybe Thisbe's a Yorkshire potbelly pig," I said, as we rested momentarily under a breadfruit tree.

"Maybe you're a male chauvinist pig," said Stephanie.

"If he is," said Rambam, "he's the only one I've ever seen with a Louis Vuitton pet carrier."

"Maybe it's time for a limerick," said Hoover, without waiting to find out. "There once was a Yorkie named Thisbee / Whose ass was as wide as a Frisbee—"

"Friedman!" shouted Stephanie. "Make him shut *up*."

"I *can't* make him shut up," I said. "Nothing can make him shut up."

"There is one thing that can make me shut up," said Hoover. "I'll shut up if anyone here can tell me the supernatural significance of the breadfruit tree, a rather hardy specimen of which is currently shading us from the sun."

"It was once a woman with big buns," said McCall, "and a big chief came by and tried to pinch a loaf and so the gal turned herself into a tree."

"Poor sap," said Rambam.

"The legend is," said Hoover, "that the breadfruit tree marks the entrance to the underworld. Its branches reach to heaven and its roots lead directly to hell, which if I'm not mistaken, is supposedly around here someplace."

"It's where we're all going," said Rambam, "if we don't get moving."

We continued along the rough and ragged route that Rambam and the Japanese innkeeper had mapped out with a little help from their friends, Hoover and the taro farmer. Again I had to wonder at the wisdom of embarking upon such a prodigious odyssey with such scant knowledge of the terrain, not to mention its supernatural underpinnings. We were about three limericks away from getting lost in the middle of a place that would've scared Hansel and Gretel right out of their cute little Teutonic outfits. Yet desperation can motivate many souls to goals they might otherwise never reach. We plodded onward, deeper into the valley of our despair.

By late that afternoon we still had not attained a visual sighting of the Hiilawe waterfall. Several of us, including myself, did, however, begin to experience a recurrent roaring in our ears that at various times we attributed to the waterfall, or to drums in the distance, or to the groaning of the spirits in the nether region of Lua O Milu. Our own spirits were groaning by this time as well. We'd taken a few small breaks in which McCall had distributed sandwiches and drinks from a knapsack, but in general it'd been pretty much balls to the wall except in Stephanie's case, of course.

By nightfall, we were zigging when we should've been zagging, crossing countless small dry riverbeds, hiking up wild goat trails, refilling canteens and thermoses at small, verdant waterfalls, careening dangerously down palis by the light of the full moon, and hoping that the roaring we now heard constantly in our ears was Hiilawe Falls and not evil spirits drinking the wind, biting themselves, and praying us to death from the ghostly branches of the next passing breadfruit tree. The moonlight made strange, spectral shadows. The dogs every once in a while would whimper at something we could not see. This never failed to send tiny processions of night marchers up and down my spine. Since morning we had seen no sign of any homo saps along the parade route. I didn't know if this was good or bad, but I found it mildly unnerving. As we plodded through the night the only constants we knew were the increasingly loud roaring in our brains that we took to be the waterfall, the eerie, penetrating, almost foreboding moonlight, and Hoover's incessant efforts at limericks, which I at least, under the circumstances, found oddly comforting for their humanity.

"A brainy young thing named DuPont," said Hoover. "Had a mind and a body she'd flaunt—"

"Make him *stop!*"

"I *can't.*"

"—in philosophy class, they pondered her ass—"

"That *bastard.*"

"—Though some claimed to favor her Kant."

The limerick brought a cool, reflexive smile to my lips in spite of myself. From Rambam, however, what started as a chuckle broke into a rather lengthy display of appreciative laughter that, I must say, did little to improve personal relations among our small group. Though no doubt exhausted by the daylong trek, Stephanie had somehow managed to build up a strong second head of steam, most of which was now being directed at the Kinkster. My protestations did little to assuage her glorious anger.

"Friedman!" she all but screamed. "I don't *need* this! The chicks don't *need* this! We're trying to find *McGovern!* We're trying to get out of here *alive!* We shouldn't have to listen to *this* shit!"

"Believe what I tell you," I shouted back. "I can't shut the little fucker up."

For Hoover's part, he'd already launched into another limerick. Fortunately, the heated exchange between Stephanie and myself had obscured the first two lines. Unfortunately, the next two came through loud and clear.

"—with a large green banana / He butt-plugged Savannah—"

Stephanie's cries of outrage and indignation carried the day only momentarily. Then, from off to the side of the trail, near a small copse covered in vines and moonlight, came another set of screams. These were somewhat deeper in tonal quality, but at least the equal of Stephanie's in terms of hysterical energy and output.

The source of the second set of screams, as we quickly discovered, was John McCall. He'd taken his own large green banana, apparently, and gone over to the left of the goat path into some foliage to urinate. As he was in the process of urinating, after the fashion of the great majority of men, his gaze did not focus upon his large green banana. Instead, he cast restless, bored, seemingly casual glances everywhere else into the area immediately around him. That was how, in fact, he'd discovered the body.

Chapter Forty

If there were four *heiaus,* or ancient temples, known to be in the Waipi'o area, several of them dating from about A.D. 680, this might indeed have been one. The foundation stones of the old structure looked as if they might've survived a similar passage of time. They'd also survived, I'm pleased to report, the passage of John McCall's translucent urine. To whiz on a *heiau,* of course, is considered an act of unparalleled desecration in Hawaii. To find behavior as spiritually callous as that, one has to go all the way back to that dark day in Texas history when Ozzy Osborne pissed on the Alamo and in so doing, pissed off every red-blooded Texas man, woman, and transsexual. The body was lying just inside the small circle of stones.

The victim was a young woman and it was clear from the numerous stab wounds in her mangled body, the dried blood on the ground, and the absence of drag marks of any kind, that she'd been done in on this site, possibly in the ritualistic sacrificial manner of countless other victims since the dawn of time. I stared down at the moonbeams gently glancing off of her sightless eyes and I realized this was the wrong way to be on the right track. The odds of finding McGovern alive had just dropped to six-to-five against.

"She couldn't've been dead long," said Rambam, studying the bloated face. "Wild pigs would've gotten her."

I felt a sweet, sad sickness inside me. Our little group had suddenly gotten very quiet. Out in the middle of this forest of evil, standing silently over the very gates of hell, I did not wish to look closely at the body. Like Thisbe and Baby Savannah, I seemed to suddenly have a mild obsession with John McCall's urine on a rock. It was not a healthy attitude, but then the world was not a healthy place. Somewhere in the near distance lurked the dark sharks who'd torn this rag doll of a girl with teeth as white as the moon. Even the waterfall seemed to be observing a moment of silence. Maybe Hiilawe had cried herself to sleep.

"Hoover," I said. "Would you please identify the body?"

Hoover was not reciting limericks any longer. He was a study in somber introspection as he stepped closer to the little floor of ancient stones. Indeed, he seemed almost mute. I thought fleetingly of something Willie Nelson had told me recently about how a kahuna had applied the age-old curse of *apo leo* upon an enemy. The curse had removed the power of speech from the victim forever. I'd told Willie to be careful the kahuna never did that to him. Willie had said he'd be very happy as an *apo leo* victim. Everybody would leave him alone and he could play golf.

"It's her," said Hoover. "It's Carline."

The rest of us would have to take his word for it; we'd never even met Carline. All I knew about her was that she'd been an indefatigable seeker of the truth as she saw it. That wasn't a bad thing to say about someone, whether alive or dead. Carline had, I suspected, come very close to getting the big story. Unfortunately, when you fly too close to the truth, it sometimes melts your wings.

We left the ruins of the young reporter in the ruins of the old temple. Sometimes that's all you can do. We were in shouting distance of the waterfall now, but nobody much felt like shouting. Hoover alone had known Carline but all of us had known and loved McGovern. That's why we were here, walking through the valley of death in the mottled moonlight like a somber procession of ghosts from the hell of our own invention. For in the sky of every friendship and every love are little tickets to hell falling like confetti from the stars. You never even see them at first. You only get one when the love or the friendship is over.

It was half-past Cinderella time when fragile, cool veils of vapor, like delicate cobwebs, signaled our approach to Hiilawe Falls. The moon was high and bright and hopeful in the way that only those who view it from a valley can know. Our hopes at finding McGovern alive, however, had been severely diminished by the macabre discovery of the body at the *heiau.* That's one of the funny things about hope. It's forever falling off that perch in your soul or being dashed to death on a rock like the tears of a princess, yet somehow it always manages to pick itself up and come right back to screw you again.

"Are you thinking what I am?" said Rambam, as the two of us held back slightly behind the rest of the group.

"Probably," I said. "What are you thinking?"

"Well, these people are pagans, right? But that doesn't mean they're stupid."

"That's right," I said. "And there's nothing more dangerous than a smart pagan."

"So they iced this reporter broad because she was getting too close to finding the sacred tampon of Queen Woo-Woo the Fourth—"

"The sacred *ka'ai,*" I corrected.

"Same thing," said Rambam, lapsing into a kind of provinciality that is endemic in New York. "And just how long do you suspect that these same people have been holding McGovern?"

"A little less than two weeks."

"I know McGovern's supposed to look like this guy Lono, but just how long do you think it's going to take these people to realize that he's not a god?"

"A little less than two hours," I said.

"That's what I'm worried about," said Rambam.

It was, indeed, the same dark thought that was on my mind. The Mayan priests had centuries ago warned that pale men would come on floating houses. They did and they killed the king and tortured half the people to death in the name of their Jesus. Now it was payback time. McGovern, very probably seduced by Carline hot on the trail of a big story, had quite involuntarily fallen into the clutches of these people. McGovern was not without charm, but, even as a housepest, two weeks was a long time for anybody not to get up your sleeve a bit. If Hoover's reporter friend had duped these people into believing that

McGovern was Lono, hoping they'd lead her to the *ka'ai,* she'd signed his death sentence as well as her own. What these people might do to McGovern would make *Deliverance* look like *Barefoot in the Park.* Quite possibly, the disaster had already occurred. Maybe we were one pale man and one floating house too late.

Chapter Forty-one

Half an hour later five people and two little dogs were paddling around in the beautiful natural wading pool surrounding the rock upon which the princess's tears had been falling for far longer than any woman should weep for any man. And while it was time for her to get over him, I wasn't going to be the one to tell her. I was looking to the east, noticing the narrow channel that provided a rare view all the way to the sea where some hours earlier, no doubt, Venus had been rising.

"Lordy!" said Stephanie, looking up in amazement. "Who put the acid in the Gatorade?"

"Almost makes you believe in God," I said.

"Or *the* gods," corrected McCall.

"I can tell you one thing," said Rambam. "You won't see this in Brooklyn."

"You won't see this anywhere on the mainland," said Hoover. "Not even Disney World. Those are lunar rainbows. There must be millions of them."

I had never heard of lunar rainbows, but even if I had, hearing about them and seeing them with your own eyes were about as different experientially as going to church was from talking directly to God over a chicken-fried steak. Even for a charismatic atheist like myself it was something of an epiphany. Now, as the moon emerged even brighter from behind a small cloud, literally millions of tiny rainbows flashed across the heavens directly above our heads. I took it as a sign.

"This has got to be the waterfall," I said, "where Kiji Hazelwood's friend found the wooden statue."

"What would a wooden statue be doing in a waterfall?" said Rambam.

"Maybe it fell off a wooden statue truck," said McCall.

"Maybe it was Kawlija the wooden Indian," said Hoover. "Maybe he was looking for his Indian maid."

I thought of Robert Louis Stevenson's poem to another princess. "And I, in her dear banyan shade, look vainly for my little maid." Hawaiian history seemed to be having a small run on brokenhearted princesses. It wasn't doing much for my mood at the moment either. If this, indeed, was the right waterfall, the one that afforded a view eastward to the sea, it was logical that this was where Kiji's friend had found the statue. Adding more credence to this theory was the fact that Carline's body was right now lying in the moonlight just down the trail from here. Carline, who'd spent five long years seeking the missing sacred *ka'ai*. Carline, who, I believed, had come very close to finding those mysterious, death-dealing relics from the beginning of time. If she hadn't come very close to finding them, she wouldn't be dead. So how *had* the wooden statue gotten into the waterfall?

In the bright moonlight I surveyed the pali over which the water was falling. It was solid, steep, sheer, and monolithic. I next turned my attention to the rock formerly known as Kakalaoa. It, too, appeared to be of one piece, mammoth in size, rubbed smooth as silk by years of tears. Did the wooden statue have brothers and sisters hiding somewhere nearby? Was it barely possible at this moment that they were rubbing shoulders with the sacred *ka'ai?*

The next thing I knew, Stephanie's voice was rising into a high wail. It stabbed like a knife through the sounds of the falling water and echoed shrilly off the white face of the pali into the darkness of the night.

"WHERE'S BABY!!" she screamed.

Chapter Forty-two

In the frantic moments that followed, we looked all around the rock and the pool for any sign of the little white Maltese. There was none. There also appeared to be no sign of Stephanie's little three-and-a-half-pound darling under the warm, translucent water, vaguely reminiscent of John McCall's urine. Baby Savannah, it seemed, had vanished from the face of the earth.

"She was just sitting on this little ledge," cried Stephanie. "Then I looked up and Baby was gone!"

There is something especially tragic about the grief of strong-willed, self-assured, world-beaters like Stephanie. The acid tongue, the youthful arrogance, the unparalleled ball-busting ability, all had vanished as suddenly as the object of her heart's affection. All that was left was a forlorn-looking little girl in a wading pool. A young princess weeping for her lost love.

"She was just sitting on this little *ledge*," Stephanie repeated, almost as if to reassure herself that there had ever been one so close to her soul.

Volunteering for submarine duty, Rambam and I both eased ourselves into the pool's sparkling water. I swam over to the ledge, a small outcropping barely above the surface of the water, almost a stepping stone to the large rock formerly known as Kakalaoa.

"She's nowhere under the surface," said Rambam, coming up for air after an underwater reconnaissance.

"She's not anywhere around the pool," said McCall, coming back from a thorough search of the perimeter.

"It was hard enough losing *Pyramus*," wailed Stephanie. "But Pyramus was *old*. Baby was only a *baby!*"

As for the ledge, it looked as desolate as a dead cheerleader's pom-pom lying in the rain. For all I could see, the game was lost. Baby herself was just about the size of a pom-pom, but while there will always be lots of pom-poms and lots of cheerleaders in this world where winning and being beautiful is everything, there was only one Baby. I doubted if Baby would've been a cheerleader anyway when she'd grown up. Now she wasn't even going to get to wear little black ribbons and attend my funeral.

It was just as I was reflecting upon this rather whimsically morbid thought that I heard it. I hadn't heard it before because it had been literally buried beneath the layers of sound emanating from the waterfall itself. But I could hear it quite plainly now as I moved closer to the ledge. A giant sucking noise like Ross Perot sucking away everybody's hopes and dreams for the future. Sure enough, hidden under the ledge was an old lava tube into whose dark interior water gushed so rapidly that had Baby been sucked out this way, she'd probably only have time for an ice-pick yelp or two before she reached the sea. Yet the hole under the ledge was the only place she could've disappeared so quickly and unaccountably. It was bad news for Stephanie, however. Anything sucked into that hole was surely a goner.

Why I did what I did next probably only Woody Allen's shrink could tell me. Maybe we all need our lost causes. Maybe it was merely a misguided effort to save all the little things in love and life that couldn't be saved. Maybe it was something as unimaginative as my wanting to go out a hero. Whatever it was, I shouted something to Rambam, words like, "If I'm not back in half an hour, I'll see you at Willie Nelson's house on Maui." Then I crawled into the hole and the water began to sweep me along like an amusement ride at a water park in hell.

The lava tube was dark and half-filled by the very cold, fast-flowing water. It was large enough for the passage of a man, and certainly a small dog, but even had I been able, it was not big enough so that I could turn around and go back. I don't know how long I rode along inside that cursed fallopian tube of mother earth, but it seemed to be eventually slanting in an upward direction and ended in a chamber of still water lighted by a small fissure of moonlight above. I walked out of the water like an evolutionary throwback into a large underground cavern lit by a series of skylights open to the moon. There was, unfortunately, no sign of Baby anywhere. The place was as quiet as a tomb, and this was not surprising, for I had every indication to believe that that was precisely what it was.

Against the dark walls of the burial cave were countless bundles of bones wrapped in tapa cloth. Giant whale teeth were suspended from the ceiling by what appeared to be braided human hair. There were capes, leis, cloaks, drums, and helmets that made the Bishop Museum look like a swap meet. There were swords made from shark's teeth and spearheads carved from what almost certainly were human bones. In this secret, long-lost place, I thought, resides the history of the Hawaiian race.

In another part of the burial cave I admired a large racing canoe that appeared to be beautifully carved from rare koa wood, which is now against the law to harvest in Hawaii, since the tree, like many aspects of the native culture, has all but disappeared. Inside the canoe, still in their proper paddling position, were three skeletons. I was in the process of absorbing this macabre spectacle when a voice very close to me almost caused me to jump through my own asshole for King Kamehameha.

"I guess they lost the race," said Rambam with a mischievous smile.

"If I knew what I was doing here," I said, once I'd discovered a shard of my composure, "I'd ask you what *you're* doing here."

"I figured if you were crazy enough to swim through that little hole, I was too. Besides, I had to get out of there. Can't stand to see a woman cry."

"You almost saw a man brown-out in his bermudas," I said. "Never sneak up on a veteran like that."

"You're a veteran all right," said Rambam. "A veteran of the Carnegie Delicatessen. Speaking of which, when do we eat? If it isn't pretty fucking soon, we might have to take a seat in one of those canoes."

"We could always catch some fish," I said, pointing to a row of what were quite obviously human jaw fishhooks with the teeth still perfectly in place.

"That's what happens when you remember to floss regularly," said Hoover, ambling slowly toward us through the gloom.

Behind him, in rapid succession, appeared McCall, and a still much-subdued Stephanie.

"I'm glad to see such a nice turnout," I said, "for our annual meeting of the Moose Lodge."

"Any sign of Baby?" asked Stephanie listlessly.

"I'm afraid not," I said. "If you'll turn your attention to the point just beyond those human skull calabashes over there, you'll find the two reasons why Baby Savannah, Carline Ravel, and yes, Mike McGovern, had to die. Two cursed, doom-laden woven baskets bearing the bones of Lono and Liloa, two high chiefs who've been dead now for over six hundred years but who've brought death and destruction over that time to anyone who consciously or unconsciously crosses their paths. Ladies and gentlemen, I give you the no-longer-missing sacred *ka'ai*."

PART NINE

On the March

Chapter Forty-three

There was something positively evil about the way the left eye of the second *ka'ai*, represented by a pearl shell, was staring at us through the dank gloom of the burial cave. After six hundred years of being shunted around, gawked at, and greedily sought after by scientists, collectors, religious fanatics, journalists, political leaders, criminals, tourists, and other curious, possessive, grasping, and anal-retentive human beings, the two caskets of bones were tired. The Holy Grail and the ark of the covenant were inanimate objects. But the sacred *ka'ai* had as much DNA still going for them as O.J. Simpson. Something about them remembered. It was not *they* who were evil, I now realized. It was not *they* who caused death and destruction. It was that dark thread of perversion that runs through the heart of every human being and leads him to look at the Elephant Man or the Wild Man from Borneo. After six hundred years the bundles of bones had finally come home and been laid to rest. We were the ones who did not belong here. The evil in the pearl shell eye was merely a reflection of ourselves, a glint of darkness from the uncharted part of the human soul.

"The first thing we do if we get out of here alive," I said, "is to forget we've ever been here."

"I'll second that," said Hoover. "The market value of the contents of this room is incalculable. The net worth of each *ka'ai*, for instance, is more than five times that of John McCall."

"That may be true," said McCall, "but how can they live like this?"

"So that's it?" said Stephanie. "We just give up on Baby? We give up on McGovern?"

"There's a time," said Rambam, not without compassion, "for us to mourn our dead. As far as McGovern's concerned, the fact that the sacred *ka'ai* are really here, I think pretty well seals his fate. Two weeks is enough to find out that anybody's not a god. But whatever they thought of McGovern, there's no way he's still alive. They couldn't take the chance. They had to kill McGovern for the same reason they had to kill Carline. To protect themselves and their precious *ka'ai.*"

"He's right," said Hoover. "If word leaked out that they'd stolen the *ka'ai* from the Bishop Museum and reburied them here, it'd start the biggest manhunt in the history of Hawaii. The entire valley would be destroyed."

"McGovern was just in the wrong place at the wrong time," I said. "He also had the wrong *face* at the wrong time. That was how this whole thing started. Carline must've tumbled some time ago to the uncanny similarities between Lono and McGovern. She was already here on the Big Island when we were putting up the handbills in Honolulu, so she probably devised the scheme early on. Back when Hoover, somewhat exaggeratively, perhaps, told her what a perfect record I had at crime-solving, she suddenly saw her chance. She seduced McGovern from the beach, seduced the locals into thinking he was Lono, and seduced me into believing that if I found the *ka'ai* I'd find my dear lost friend McGovern."

"What about Baby?" Stephanie persisted.

"You want the truth?" said Rambam. "Baby weighs about five pounds—"

"Baby weighs three and a half pounds," said Stephanie staunchly.

"Okay," said Rambam. "Three and a half pounds. She was probably tossed like a twig into a side channel and swept out to sea. I'm really sorry but that's how it is."

"There are times in all our lives," I said quietly, "when we must lose our little Malteses and our favorite Irish poets. We'll never get over; we'll just get above—"

"Shut *up*, Dickhead!" said Stephanie. "I *heard* something."

I pulled my lips together and the five of us listened intently. Sure enough, a barely discernible sound, almost like faraway music in the wind, seemed to be filtering its way into the burial cave. Then the wind must have shifted, because the music suddenly became louder, the words clearly audible to us all.

Tall and tan and young and lovely
The girl from Ipanema goes walking . . .

"Jesus Christ!" I ejaculated. "That's McGovern's fucking tape!"

Frantically, we stumbled through the twilight in the direction of the music, I being a little behind the others since Stephanie had just handed me a sopping wet Thisbe in her Louis Vuitton pet-carrier. Hoover found the exit first, a small crevice in the side of the cave, only wide enough for one person at a time to squeeze through.

After a small eternity, we found ourselves jumbled together upon a narrow, dusty canyon floor. At the other end of the canyon was a small fire with what appeared to be tiny figures gathered about it. The music was plainly coming from the far end of the canyon.

As we ran rapidly down the dry riverbed, *The Girl from Ipanema* echoing off the palis, we could easily see that one figure appeared to be much larger than the others. As we moved still closer, we saw that the figures were dancing. The image of McGovern became quite clear to us, wearing some kind of native loincloth, balancing what looked like a pineapple on his head, and dancing with what appeared to be several bare-breasted, nubile young girls in very tiny grass skirts. We stopped for a moment to take in the pure pagan joy of the little scene.

"I think I was at that table twenty years ago," said McCall, shaking his head enviously.

"For somebody who's supposed to be dead," said Rambam, "he certainly seems to be making the most of it."

"*The Man Who Would Be King*," I said.

"Will you look at the honkers on those wahines!" said Hoover admiringly.

"Hoover!" said Stephanie. "McGovern's *alive* and all you can do is talk about half-naked women?"

"All right," said Hoover. "Will you look at the honkers on those wahines who happen to be gyrating around McGovern!"

"So that's what they're calling it these days," said Rambam.

Because of the loud music, or maybe because he was bombed out of his skull, or maybe because he was so thoroughly enjoying gyrating with the large-honkered wahines, McGovern still as yet had not detected our arrival. We had long since tired of running down the riverbed shouting, "McGovern! You're alive!" Now we had slowed to a more reasonable pace, considering the day's exertions, and we contented ourselves with watching McGovern at play, the way doting parents might approvingly watch over a happy child.

What happened next, however, was every parent's nightmare. It started with a long line of torches suddenly materializing and moving silently down the steep zigzag trail of the pali. The fabled deadly night marchers seemed to be headed directly toward McGovern.

Chapter Forty-four

The Girl from Ipanema had walked to the sea and now Frank Sinatra's perfectly phrased cadences of *New York, New York* were echoing off the palis into the blameless tropical sky. We watched in horror, like those who witness an automobile accident in the making and can do nothing to stop it. The line of ghostly silent torch-bearers now extended almost the full length of the pali, and still McGovern and his dancing girls remained totally oblivious to their impending peril. It was mesmerizing, maddening, and macabre, like watching a horrible dream or a poison flower unfolding inexorably in slow motion. Then came the drums.

They were like no drums I had ever heard before. Carried by the tide and the wind and the stars through the cathedral night, they seemed to catch and hold and verily become the pounding of the human heart. Ole Blue Eyes and his vagabond shoes were out of there now. The entire valley was gripped with a transcendental terror, a morbid, fearful fascination, like an insect freezing in place before being devoured by some unfathomable crepuscular monster.

We huddled behind a small ledge and watched McGovern and the girls huddling beside the small fire. There was no way to get to them in time and there was nothing to do even if we'd gotten there. In truth, there was no way to move at all. For their part, McGovern and his native friends now seemed to be painfully aware of the dark destiny approaching them. The girls, indeed, soon vanished like so many chameleons into the nearby protective foliage, leaving only McGovern standing stoic and calm like the giant that he was, to face the true terror of what one's brain denies to be true while one's blood screams out it's for real.

"Can't we do *anything* to help him?" whispered Stephanie. Thisbe whimpered at her side.

"When the night marchers come for you like that," said Hoover, "your number's really up. We can only hope that the girls told McGovern what to do. It's the only hope he has."

The line of marchers had now reached the dusty canyon floor, obscuring McGovern from our view. They looked like ghostly, ghastly, out-of-focus warriors wearing helmets and feathered capes like the ones we'd seen in the burial cave. Some carried spears as well as torches. Their spears and capes and helmets were easily definable, but their faces looked oddly like figures viewed through a frosted window in the mental hospital of a dream.

And now, as we huddled behind the ledge, the night marchers began chanting. Thousands of disembodied voices chanting as one to the perfect, puissant, pagan rhythms of the drums of doom. The air in the little valley grew noticeably colder. Clouds covered the moon. The marchers continued onward in a relentless line past the place where McGovern had been and no longer could be descried.

"Poor McGovern," said Stephanie softly. "He's with Baby now. Across the rainbow bridge."

There was nothing to add to that and none of us tried. In time, the night marchers marched on to other plains and other lands. In time, the valley filled again with bright moonlight as the dark clouds hurried across the silver stars to other heavens and other skies. The night air grew warm again and redolent with the lingering perfume of the islands. But there was no sign, as we moved carefully across the canyon floor, of McGovern or the native girls or the fire that we'd seen earlier. The only fire now was the one in our hearts. In mine, burned a sad and lonely flame. Far from warming my spirit, it merely reminded me that life hangs by spit and all great love is hopeless.

We were tired, dispirited, and emotionally exhausted by the time we'd reached the far end of the rocky riverbed. To let us find McGovern only to watch him die seemed like one of God's cruel tricks that He sometimes in His divine perversion plays upon hapless human beings. It was akin to showing Moses the Promised Land but not permitting him to go there. Or not letting Stanley Kubrick make it to 2001. What the hell, I thought. A sick sense of humor's better than none at all.

The ashes were cold by the time we reached McGovern's little campfire. No McGovern, of course. No girls. No joy.

"Aren't these fucking night marchers at least supposed to leave behind their victims' bodies?" asked Rambam, as we made a cursory search of the area.

"You wouldn't think anybody would try to carry McGovern too far," said McCall.

I was just ready to turn back when a shiny glint of light manifested itself in my peripheral vision. I walked over to inspect it further and was somewhat taken back by the nature of the object. Then I literally jumped for joy. It was McGovern's large white luminous buttocks reflecting in the moonlight.

"Are they gone yet?" he said.

I had to admit it was a memorable sight peering into a small depression by the wall of the canyon and seeing McGovern's enormous form lying prostrate on the ground stark naked. Once everyone saw that he was all right, they all reacted in kind.

"Hell of a way to receive company," said Rambam.

"This calls for a little celebratory verse," said Hoover. "There once was a limerist named Hoover / Who got his dick caught in a louver—"

"McGovern *could* use a little work in the gym," interrupted McCall.

"I'm going to give you a big hug," said Stephanie, "but first you have to put your loincloth back on. That's absolutely disgusting."

"Are they gone yet?" said McGovern.

In fairly short order McGovern got up, got dressed after a fashion, and expressed a desire to have a big, hairy steak in Honolulu. Because of McGovern's recent rather traumatic experience, and our own perilous adventures of the past twenty-four hours, I decided to postpone the debriefing process on McGovern. The postmortem could come later. I was just glad it wasn't going to be a postmortem on McGovern's body.

"What I don't understand," said Rambam, "is *why* the night marchers didn't kill McGovern?"

"That's easy," I said. "The only people they're known to occasionally spare are children. In McGovern, their supernatural sensibilities no doubt picked up on his childlike, Peter Pan–like, thoroughly irritating innocence."

"There *are* some advantages," said McGovern, "to being me."

McGovern followed us like a little puppy back to the campfire area and I noted with some poignancy as he gathered his possessions that they were only two in number: his fucking tape and a large carved coconut.

"Where'd you get the coconut?" asked Rambam.

"One of the girls gave it to me as a gift," said McGovern, "just before the night marchers crashed our little party."

McGovern looked at the rather ornately carved object for a moment. Then he handed it to Stephanie.

"I'll give it to you," he said. "You look so beautiful in the moonlight."

"That's sweet, McGovern," said Stephanie.

"Open it up," said McGovern.

As Stephanie removed the top half of the coconut, without hesitation, Baby Savannah jumped into her arms. There were tears on Stephanie's face and I might add, on a few other faces as well.

"Oh, darling!" she said. "You found McGovern!"

PART TEN

On the Other Hand

Chapter Forty-five

Two nights and countless penis coladas later, at a small table under a million stars, Hoover, McGovern, and myself were admiring the music and the hula dancers at the Tahitian Lanai in Honolulu. McCall, Rambam, and Stephanie had all departed, giving the same lame excuse that they had to get back to their lives on the mainland. McGovern, Hoover, and I didn't have lives so we didn't really give a damn where we didn't live them. At the moment, the scenery, both man-made and natural, looked pretty good.

"I am the Lindbergh baby!" shouted McGovern to a beautiful, if somewhat bewildered hula dancer. She recovered quickly, however, favoring him with a beautiful smile and personally placing a lei around his neck without missing a beat.

The story of McGovern's adventures had taken a while for Hoover and I to piece together but when it all came out it was pretty much what I'd expected. It had all been fairly incestuous. Hoover had shown pictures of McGovern and myself on a previous trip to Carline Ravel at the same time as he was touting my infallible investigative abilities to her. She'd not only been impressed with me but, being an expert on Hawaiian history, she'd also recognized the uncanny likeness between McGovern and Lono. She'd proceeded to provide McGovern with his ticket to Hawaii.

"If I'd only kept my mouth shut," said Hoover, "she might be alive today."

"Not a chance," I said. "She merely would've found another way of tracking down the missing *ka'ai*. And without her blazing the trail, no one would've ever known their whereabouts. In a sense she did succeed in uncovering one of the greatest stories in the history of mankind—the existence and location of the burial caves of the ancient Hawaiians."

"And in spite of my basic reporter instincts,"said Hoover, "my human instincts dictate that that story will never see the light of day. It'd be a little bit like steppin' on a rainbow."

"Hear! Hear!" shouted McGovern, in obvious heartfelt agreement. "I'm proud of you, Hoover. Knowing when *not* to break a story is the hardest judgement call a journalist ever has to make. History will remember you as a good and wise man."

"But I'll remember Hoover as something else," I said.

"You will?" said Hoover.

"But, of course!" I said, rather magnanimously.

"How will you remember him?" asked McGovern, with almost childlike sincerity.

"As the boy who travels with me," I said.

We ordered another round of drinks and took in the thatched roofs and the piano bar and the dancers and the stars. But something was still worrying Hoover.

"When Carline called Kinky in New York with the 'Hang loose. Lono is home,' message, where were you, McGovern?"

"I was right next to her at the Hilo Airport."

"Why did you add the MIT—MIT—MIT?" Hoover wanted to know.

"Because," said McGovern, "I didn't know if I was in trouble or not. I've been looking for the answer to that question ever since I was a kid. I guess I haven't been looking too hard, though. I've just been wandering in the raw poetry of time."

Sometime later, after a particularly animated discussion, Hoover and I glanced around and abruptly discovered that the two of us were now the only occupants at the table.

"Jesus Christ, Kinkyhead," said Hoover in some exasperation. "*Now* where the hell has McGovern disappeared to?"

I looked at the sea. I looked at the sky. I looked back at Hoover.

"Don't ask," I said.